LINDA LEATHERBARROW

Essential Kit

LINDA LEATHERBARROW

Essential Kit

L. Leatherbarrow

MAIA

Published in 2004 by
The Maia Press Limited
82 Forest Road
London E8 3BH
www.maiapress.com

Earlier versions of these stories have appeared in various publications:
'Ride': *The Bridport Prize Anthology* 2001; *Even the Ants have Names* 2002
'Essential Kit': *The Sunday Express Magazine* 2002
'Shush': *Mslexia Magazine* 2003
'Gorilla': *Ambit* 1998 and *New Writing 8* 1999
'The Student': *Even the Ants have Names* 2002
'La Luna': *The Nerve* 1998
'Lost Boys': *Harlot Red* 2001
'Crime in a Fairy-tale Forest': *Matter* 2004

ISBN 1 904559 10 7

A CIP catalogue record for this book is available from the British Library

Printed and bound in Great Britain by Thanet Press

Contents

▼

Ride

IF YOU TAKE THE TUBE to Victoria, longing to be out of this hazy city, to be on your own, where each step is a miracle of moving forward with no side-stepping or going round, the line of your thoughts staying in line with your feet, if you trek up the escalator, adjust your backpack for the fourth time, take a swig from your water-bottle, then pass through the shiny new shopping mall, smelling of melting chocolate, go out at the back and cross Buckingham Palace Road, smelling of fried sunlight, you will come to Victoria Coach Station and, if you slog through Departures, dodging bodies draped across the floor, sleeping or otherwise, trying not to tread on feet, hands, suitcases, pigeons, or empty crisp packets, you will come to Bay 19 where, because you are forty minutes early, being the sort of person who cannot stand being late, you will find yourself in a privileged position, sitting on the front seat of the Glasgow coach, to the left of the driver and behind the big front window, where you can stretch your legs and nibble peanut butter and cucumber sandwiches, Battenberg cake, hard-boiled eggs and tangerines, thoughtfully provided for you by Mum, who obviously has no sense of smell and worries that you would have tried to last out the journey solely on a packet of chewing gum (and she'd be right; just the thought of a hard-boiled egg makes you heave), and where you can stare straight ahead at the road, at unimpeded vistas of land-scapes to come, savage yellow rectangles of oilseed rape, the smear of cities tucked into distant folds, and, closer up, splattered bugs on your window and an Uncle Bulgaria womble swinging by its scarf from the central mirror like a felon from a gibbet, making you think of death and, because there is really no point in thinking about death (it's not going to change anything, is it?) and because death is pretty much the same as divorce, Dad going off to Birmingham to live with his boyfriend and stepping right off the planet, or might just as well have for all you've seen of him, and because you don't want to be thinking about this (again), you consider digging out of your anorak pocket your second-hand cloth-bound volume of Heidegger's *Being and Time* but it seems pretentious, risky even, and you wish you'd brought *Man and Boy* by Tony Parsons which someone at work recommended last week, though you hate Tony Parsons and think he's a jerk, only watching him on *The Late Show* because it's important to keep up so you've got something to talk about at work (you have a Saturday job at Dixon's, Wood Green) and, because you're always slightly in love with older men, especially those with Irish brogues and thinning hair who know far more than you will ever know – knowledge being like slate-grey lentils bought from a Turkish grocer's, trickling through your fingers until only the gravel bits are left behind – you decide to talk to the driver though there is a notice, right in front of you, saying Do Not Talk To The Driver, but you do anyway and discover his name is Marty, that he plays trumpet for the Salvation Army, lives in Southampton and has already been driving all night and this is overtime (not strictly allowed) and you tell him that your name is Mira Rainbird, that you're doing an extra year at school in order to re-take your A Levels, are going to walk the entire West Highland Way by yourself, and that you, that is Mum, owns a West Highland terrier called Steed – after Steed in *The Avengers* – then, when you're halfway up the motorway, Marty pulls over into the slow lane, clicks on his microphone to address all the passengers, not just you, and asks that they join with him in thanking their Maker that they have not *yet* arrived at the Pearly Gates, are not *yet* asking St Peter's permission to pass through, unlike that lot in the other coach who passed through earlier, remember? (how could you forget when you and Marty had a full-on view?) that lot who skidded on an oil patch, smashed into the central barricade, zigzagged then mounted the bank, rolled down the other side into a reservoir and drowned, all of them, including the driver (Marty knows that this is what happened after they disappeared over the bank because control have been on to him on the radio, checking if he got clear or is stuck in tailback) and, by now, you're thinking about bits of bodies, two fingers picked up in a glove, people wrapped in weed, down in the mud where they sink deeper and deeper until their flesh becomes mud, their bones piled hugger-mugger like the bones of all those people at Vesuvius, and you're wondering why people would choose to live on the skirts of a volcano, thinking about a programme on BBC Knowledge that you sat up watching late last night, with Mum, when you should have been going to bed early so as to be fresh for the journey, a programme called *The Boiling Seas*, which took nearly an hour to get to the boiling part and was mostly to do with carbon dioxide being taken up by the Amazon rainforest and stored, and it's possible you fell asleep because, apart from the title shot of flames licking waves, you can't remember any boiling, and now Marty is asking that we thank God for saving us from the fate that befell the three young soldiers, remember? (this you didn't see, passing by shortly after it happened) three young soldiers who were crushed in the back of their jeep by a Sainsbury's lorry, its driver falling asleep at the wheel just before Rugby, and here you can't help wondering (again) if it was entirely prudent of Marty to have used up all his legal driving miles last night and how much sleep-deprivation is endemic among long-distance drivers and, meanwhile, Marty is explaining that he is a first-timer, straight out of training school, who has never before driven a coach all the way up the M6 from London to Glasgow, and that there should be a co-driver to keep him company and take a turn at the wheel, only he called in sick and it's illegal for him (Marty) to drive for more than four hours without a comfort break but what can you do in these circumstances and so far so good, eh folks? and there is a ragged cheer of acknowledgement then one of the passengers – Robby from Swansea – comes down the gangway to ask if he can take the microphone to say something on behalf of his fellow passengers and Marty says it's irregular but, sure, why not? and you think this is *so* embarrassing and cringe back into your seat and wish, momentarily, that you were not at the front, out in the open, where Robby, who has something wrong with his nose which makes it look as if a war has been fought over every pore, and something wrong with his genitals which roll inside his trousers like a rugger-ball, sprays you with saliva as he adds his, and everybody else's, thanks to those expressed before, remarking that in spite of not being able to take a comfort break on this epic, and he does mean *epic* journey, Marty has driven like a hero, and he does mean *hero*, and he has no doubt that we will, eventually, reach Glasgow, in spite of delays, tailbacks, thunderstorms, floods, thirty-two miles of traffic cones near Watford, the fallen bridge at Coventry, and he talks on, listing and spewing like a drunken missionary, clutching the microphone, swaying with the motion of the coach, now doing eighty-eight miles per hour (you can see the speedo), gabbling on in spite of the notice which says Strictly No Standing Beside The Driver until, blushing, he wipes his forehead with a white cotton handkerchief with an R embroidered in one corner, and retires to his seat in a volley of claps and cheers and a feeble rendition of *For He's A Jolly Good Fellow*, started up by Monica at the back, whose enormous chest is falling out of her scoop-neck shocking pink T-shirt emblazoned with the legend Eyes Off Dick-Head, who now comes forward to offer Marty a little something from her hip flask, just to keep you going, darling, everyone needs a little something to keep them going, in spite of the notice saying It Is An Offence To Consume Alcohol On This Vehicle, and Marty, having said earlier that anyone found drinking will be forcibly removed, who now says he doesn't mind if he does, and so do you, and soon there's a party going on, and you're more relieved than you can say that you kept the Heidegger in your pocket and didn't let on for a moment that you're the sort who reads; a party just at the front, you understand, because, at the back, some passengers are trying to sleep and someone's baby is almost murdered by a medical student who is revising for his exams (which he has to sit tomorrow), and you're secretly in sympathy with him because you think, if you ever had a baby yourself, and you're sure you wouldn't but, if you ever did, you'd be the sort who would shake it and kill it and have to stand trial for homicide or babycide, or whatever, and you imagine the baby's coffin, immaculate with heaped-up white lilies with fat orange stamens dripping brick-red pollen over the sides, until it's stained and streaked like a tiger coffin – a tiger-cub coffin – and, while you're imagining it going down, past the plastic grass, into the worm-wriggling earth, the mother wallops the student with a Nike sports bag containing thirty-six disposable nappies, thirty of which are still clean, two packets of baby wipes, four full bottles of formula milk and two empty ones, six brand-new Babygros and a silver foil twist of black ganja which the man in her health-food store promised is the very best, a coming-home present for her boyfriend – if the baby will only just go to sleep and stay alive and keep breathing, if he (the student) will keep his filthy mitts to himself and stop eyeing her up and shouting at the baby, who is only crying after all, which is what babies do, isn't it? and what does he think she can do about it, stuck on the coach like this without a break? and now there is a bit of a riot with five or six of the passengers coming forward to say Stop The Coach, and Marty saying that he's Only Doing His Job (you can hear the capitals) and he can't let them off, even if we *are* stationary, and to use the chemical toilet at the rear, and someone shouting that that's not a chemical toilet but a cesspit and a health hazard and if Marty doesn't stop the coach *this instant* he will open the emergency door because there is someone here who is *seriously* travel sick and is going to throw up,

correction *has* thrown up, so LET US OFF but Marty grinds
into gear again, lurches forward, and you wonder if he's
planning to go up the backside of the car transporter in
front, or over the Mini with the little kiddies inside, sticking
their fingers up at him and blowing raspberries, and, at this
point, you realise just how much you're enjoying yourself
and wish you could be on this coach forever, the air rich
with blasphemy and swearing, the clear promise of violence,
the smell of Marty's sweat, ripe as the smell of the hard-
boiled egg which, somehow, you're eating because it's
getting dark and you're beginning to think about morning
and how far away it is and whether, when you're this
far north, past Wigan, it stays lighter at night and there
might be an aurora borealis, like in *Local Hero* when Burt
Lancaster tells his anger therapist to fuck off and flies from
his global headquarters in Houston, Texas, to the northerly
tip of Scotland because he's obsessed with comets and all
things astronomical, where you can see every star because
the air is so clean, the light so pellucid, where you're going
(if you ever get off this coach), and you keep looking straight
ahead through your big front window because it is yours
now, only yours and Marty's, the others having given up and
gone back, sulking and smoking in spite of the notice saying
No Smoking, and you're beginning to worry about passive
smoking and Marty says it's a shame about the air condi-
tioning, he doesn't know why they build these coaches with
windows that can't be opened, a shame, on his first trip and
all, it's enough to put you off, and he should have stuck it
out at his last job which turns out to have been guarding
offenders in Brixton nick, and you begin to wonder about
the word offender and who is offended and why, until you're

almost on the point of digging out the Heidegger seeing that, now it's dark, no one will notice you reading and, anyway, half of them are asleep, when you notice how beautiful it's getting, tail lights up ahead spilling over the hills, streams of lights flying up, streams of lights falling down, and all the things you can't see are simply blacker parts of the night and you're riding, in this great illuminated vehicle, like an exile riding into a country you thought you'd never see again, because, although you haven't been to Scotland, your mother was born there; it's in the blood and London is just the place you live; or rather, instead of an exile, you're a ghost who's forgotten who it was but pines to be back, until, after all, none of this matters because you're too busy soaking up the atmosphere of concentration, duty and responsibility, bravely borne by Marty, and it's as if you and Marty are one and it's up to you to deliver the passengers safely to their destination, passengers who are melding and sinking together in the treacle blackness, mouths open, arms loose, the coach warm with the breath of their sleeping; even the mother of the almost-murdered baby is sleeping, her baby sleeping in the nest of her arms, and, on the seat beside them, the medical student, also sleeping, dreams of attending a dissection in St Bartholomew's Hospital, the body on the table recently dug up from its grave and carried into the hospital in a laundry basket (he will write about this in his exam tomorrow and lose marks for digression), while, on the fourth row from the back, Robby from Swansea, neither dreaming nor sleeping, stares out of his side window at the flicking trace-lines of hedges, branches leafed with rooks waiting for daybreak and thermals that will rise from the morning tarmac, and thinks that it has been a good journey, in spite of everything, and that he has distinguished himself, yes he means *distinguished*, in coming forward to speak up for them all, in being the kind of person who seizes the moment and talks into microphones, and thinks that, tomorrow, he will ask for promotion and, even if he doesn't get it, it will be enough to know that he asked, and, on the seat behind his, Monica sleeps with her mouth open, her generous chest rising and falling like an ocean becalmed, while you sit back on the front seat, entirely awake, having eaten the peanut butter sandwiches and given some of your Battenberg to Marty, (thanks very much, don't mind if I do) and wonder if, on the way back, you might hop off at Birmingham because there is nothing to stop you calling in on Dad and, anyway, it might be preferable to catch him on *his* patch rather than wait forever for him to haul himself down to London where he could bump into Mum, then you peel a tangerine, watch the lights of faraway places and a silver quarter-moon skipping from left to right of the coach then back again, the road bending while appearing to be straight, and think this is grand, this being away from home, this being on your own for the first time, truly on your own.

Rescue

▼

THAT NIGHT, I was coming home late, not exceptionally late but most of the lights in the town were out, the streets empty. I wasn't drunk enough to find this forbidding or even sad, just sufficiently sloshed to make my progress along Applemore Street a shade more calculated than normal. It was extremely cold, the temperature plummeting and in the morning there would undoubtedly be a hard frost.

It was my birthday and I'd been celebrating with Sinclair Stanley. He was a rude old sod, but I was fond of him and, that night, he was on form, using my birthday as an excuse to launch into an examination of my career to date, and in particular my future prospects.

'James,' he said, 'don't pretend that you're busy.'

Both of us had retired five years ago, Sinclair from his duties as Headmaster of St Katherine's College and me from a lifetime of inspecting schools. Sinclair had some idea that we might write a book together.

I was thinking about this as I made my way past shuttered shops and empty alleyways, not drawn to the project, wanting to put aside assessment and syllabuses, but not entirely averse. I did have something to say on the subject and so did Sinclair. On Betterton Road, I crossed over at the park. The gaps between the trees made me nervous. Ours is a relatively safe town, but a singleton like me, whose steps were not entirely taking the straightest line, would be an easy target. I was looking forward to my bed, not that I would sleep when I got there, even though I'd treated myself the week before to a new goose-down duvet in the sales. I never managed more than three or four hours. The World Service was my companion, Sinclair and the World Service, not a lonely life but restricted.

If I hadn't crossed the road, I wouldn't have gone past the phone box, possibly the last traditional solid red phone box in the town. A sound appeared to be coming from inside which I couldn't immediately identify, a faint mewling and yowling, a stray cat or wounded seagull perhaps, and I was half inclined to leave it for someone else to deal with in the morning.

'Seize the moment,' Sinclair had said, pouring us both a brandy.

'What moment?'

'Whichever one comes along,' he said.

I stood on the kerb and hesitated. 'For goodness sake,' I said. Wrapped up in himself you might say, up his own arse, and you'd be right, like most elderly people who live on their own. Elderly was a word I was trying out to see if it could plausibly be considered in relationship to myself. 'An elderly gentleman,' I said out loud, swaying slightly and taking hold of the phone box to steady myself, 'retiree, old codger,' then there it was again and this time, I did what any more alert and generous person would have done five minutes earlier: I opened the door and entered the phone box.

At first I didn't know what to make of it – the usual smell of piss and the receiver dangling on the end of the wire like a man dangling on a noose, nothing else except a Tesco carrier bag on the floor. The mewling sound had stopped and I was about to leave when the bag twitched, then, out poked the smallest hand you could imagine, a crumpled red hand with a bracelet of mottled red flesh round the wrist, nails like flakes of pearl.

I was sobering up fast. Maybe the cold had cleared my head. Bending down, I put out a finger to stroke it. I did this without thinking, an instinctual thing, and it responded in kind, twisting and grasping my finger. Foxy red hair, creamy skin, eyes closed, mouth open, a baby wearing nothing but a chenille velvet scarf, the sort of thing women wear to parties to cheer up a black dress they've worn once too often, a gold scarf with embroidery and sequins. There is little warmth in chenille velvet so I drew the baby out of the bag, took off my own dark blue woollen scarf, and wrapped it over the gold and glitter.

It was the first time I'd ever held a baby and I was taken aback – instant tenderness mixed with anger for the person who had left it there, a terror that it might die in my arms, and a strange connectedness. The baby was still clutching my finger when it opened its eyes – black eyes that stared at me without blinking, and took hold of me. It happened so quickly and I was reminded of a book I'd read years ago by Konrad Lorenz, about some experiments he did with goslings. The first thing the goslings saw when they came out of the egg was Mother. It didn't matter if it was a three-legged dog or a shopping trolley, they'd form an orderly line and follow it wherever it went. I'd been imprinted, I didn't doubt it, but it was rather unsettling because, although the baby had claimed me, I knew that this was only temporary.

It was going to have to make adjustments later and Heaven only knew what that might do to its developing psyche. Not my problem, I told myself. Somewhere at the back of my brain, old Sinclair was muttering.

'Shut up,' I told him.

I slipped the baby inside my coat, next to my chest, then bent down again, picked up the carrier bag with my free hand, crumpled it up and stuffed it into my coat pocket. I don't know why I did this, perhaps in case it contained clues, perhaps, though I only thought of this later, to conceal evidence, then I stepped out of the phone box and began to walk down Betterton Road. The police station was a mile away on the other side of the town and the hospital about two miles away, beyond the outskirts. There was no debate. Sinclair could mutter as much as he liked. Ethics might once have been his subject but this wasn't a question of ethics. It had nothing to do with right or wrong; this was a straightforward question of the law.

I walked towards the police station as fast as I could, my head scrambled with questions. How could anyone do such a thing? Why would they? How old was the baby? How long had it been there in the cold? Who had put it there and did they regret it already? I began to run, clutching the baby under my coat, terrified that, unaccustomed to running, I might fall over and drop it. Everything went out of my head, Sinclair, our evening together, my life, his life; there was only this terrible urgency, my feet striking the hard pave-ment on behalf of someone else. And I thought about what Rose might have done. The same as me – wrapped it up, put it under her coat. Of course she would. It was what anyone would do. No one could leave it there to freeze. I hadn't thought of her today, a whole day without her, which was most unusual. She would have loved a baby but they wouldn't let her adopt – 'too old,' they said – and now I was carrying one, a boy or a girl, I didn't know, didn't care, warming it up, carrying it to safety, poor little thing. I was carrying it for *her*. Which made me tearful and I realised how sentimental and ridiculous I was being, a wallowing old widower. How selfish. This was about the baby, not me. What kind of a life would it have, abandoned like this? Who would look after it? Its heart beat next to my heart and I saw nothing but misery ahead of it, the social services doing their careful best, the children's homes, the foster homes. My head filled up with tabloid rubbish – sexual abuse, beatings. What kind of a start was that?

I ran on and it began to rain, a freezing sleet that hurled itself at my open throat and bit into my face, so that I hunched deeper into my coat, put up the collar, my face and the baby's face very close, its eyes still fixed on mine. The movement must have quietened it – the rushing, the night, my footsteps on the pavements, my body pounding along on its behalf. Maybe the movement reminded it of the womb it had so recently left. Maybe it realised it was safe. It was warmer too, surely it was warmer, please God it was warmer, but what if it were hungry?

I knew nothing about babies but I felt sure it would be hungry. What did I have at home? I had to go past my road on the way to the police station and, in a few more minutes, I'd be there. The central heating was on, there was milk in the fridge, it made sense. I could telephone the police and they could come when the baby was fed. What the baby needed immediately was warmth and food. It didn't need officialdom and form-filling. It didn't need a wait while they checked out the phone box or called for an ambulance. I flew along with the baby snuggled in tight. 'It's all right,' I told it and tried to remember a lullaby but failed. I'm not sure lullabies were in my mother's repertoire. Anyway, I managed a few lines of *Greensleeves* which seemed to settle it.

There were blue streaks in the sky where the edge of the sea lay below the roofs. I staggered up the steps. The town is built into a cliff and there are steps everywhere. It isn't a town for the elderly. The houses sink together, roofs sag, walls bow, the windows are filmy and partitioned with lead. It isn't a town for a child. Not unless he or she is interested in history. The thought came into my head and wouldn't dislodge. What kind of a child was I carrying under my coat? What if it were a clever child and no one gave it any books?

I was going up and up, wondering for the millionth time why I'd bought this big house on top of the town, with all its empty rooms. I reminded myself that it used to be a happy house when *she* was there. I laboured up the hill and the baby, so small under my coat, so tucked in, began to cry again, a terrible bleating sound that I couldn't bear. It was crying and there was no one there to hear it except myself. By this time I was running slower, gasping for breath, the pavements yellow, the hedges black, a cat shooting out from under a car and nearly tripping me up, my legs dragging and heavy as if they belonged to someone else, but I had to keep going. I had to get the baby out of the cold, get some food down its gullet, dilute a little milk with water, warm it up. If I dipped my finger in the milk and put it in the baby's mouth, would it suck? Of course it would. As soon as it was comfortable, I'd telephone the police.

But what if I didn't? What if a man were to bring it up as his own? Who would stop him? There would have to be lies, inventions, perhaps a daughter in New Zealand by a former marriage never spoken about, a daughter with a late baby, a daughter who'd died tragically in a car crash, ditto the baby's father. I imagined myself explaining this to Sinclair. 'No other grandparents,' I'd say, 'so I have to look after it. Of course it won't be easy but what else can I do?' And there was Sinclair, handing me a glass of dessert wine and a Cantuccini biscuit to dunk, saying, 'Of course, of course, James, you're doing the right thing.' As for officialdom and their precious bits of paper, I could fabricate something – you could make anything look good with a computer and a photocopier these days – a birth certificate that would pass muster couldn't be that difficult and the baby would be an adult before it came up against the heavy stuff – National Insurance numbers, passports. By then it could look after itself.

I knew, of course, that this was only a fantasy. I was going to keep running up the hill and down the other side, along Redmond Road, across Market Street to the police station. I was going to hand over the baby and say goodbye. I was going to hand over the baby and put the whole episode firmly out of my mind.

Sinclair kept butting in and I kept telling him to keep quiet.

'It's your birthday,' he said. 'Remember?'

I took the short cut past the back of Carpet Warehouse, past the loading bay and over the car park. I'd forgotten about my birthday but there it was. We shared a birthday. If you were a boy, you could have my first name. If you were a girl, my second. James Caroline, a name I've never liked but which in certain situations has obvious advantages. Dream on, I thought. The police would take you to the hospital, of course they would, and the nurses would give you a name – probably Angel, something undignified and soppy that you would have to struggle against all your life. Along with everything else. The sleet was turning to snow and it was bitterly cold. No baby should be out in weather like that. I would have to take you home; it was the safest thing to do and your safety came first. As soon as I had you settled, I could log on and get Tesco's to send round whatever you needed in the morning – baby milk, nappies, pyjamas. A big house, a big garden to play in, a high wall all round it. Nowhere could be safer. Up the hill, up the steps, my heart going like the clappers. Through the gate. Why did it always stick? Why hadn't I oiled it? Quick, fish out the key, open the door, in before anyone sees us.

Essential Kit

▼

YOU'RE WALKING the West Highland Way. On your own. Which is how you want it, never mind that Mum worries, Dad panics – they'll have to get used to it, and, besides, they're talking now for the first time in years. Walk all day, stop where you like, sleep in the tent, everything you need on your back, but, after five days of a thundery black mass that won't clear up, the wind chucking rain straight in your face, you break your first rule, decide to stay in a bed-and-breakfast. If you can find one.

Four miles further on, you squint through the torrent at a double-fronted white cottage huddling in a clump of beech trees. Hood down, you stagger up the path, ring the bell, and are shown upstairs by a tiny woman in a Nike tracksuit. Her name is Jolly and she talks to you in a language you can't understand, which could be Bangladeshi Glaswegian, or Gujarati Aberdonian. On second thoughts it's definitely Glaswegian – more Glaswegian than *Taggart*.

It's quiet, very quiet. Maybe you're the only guest. You dump your rucksack, tip your kit on to the floor, tug off your boots, stretch your sodden sleeping bag over the backs of two chairs, and unpeel your clothes – Orkney storm jacket, Outer Hebrides fleece, Whirlwind micro-fleece, Monsoon over-trousers, Eclipse trousers, Northern Lights wicking

33

T-shirt, Cloud Walker trekking socks, Cloud Walker lining socks – spread them along the radiators then crawl into bed in your windproof knickers.

In the morning, you have a shower in the en-suite, haul on your clothes – piping hot, bone dry – then slip downstairs to catch breakfast in an empty dining room; empty that is of other diners, otherwise crowded. Every shelf, nook, niche and window sill is adorned with naked ladies: naked ladies standing under fibre-optic waterfalls, naked ladies holding Olympic torches, naked ladies riding bare-back on Alsatian dogs, on mirror-work cows and sandalwood elephants. Why do people have all this . . . this *stuff*?

Jolly appears in a turquoise sari and you let her know that you're vegetarian and it turns out that she is too and doesn't do bacon, sausages, kidneys or black pudding. You eat fifteen miles' worth of Shredded Wheat then settle up and check out the essential gifts in a little alcove off the hall. Normally you hate shopping but you must buy something; you could be the only customer she's had all week, all year.

'Please,' she says, ushering you in. 'A little souvenir for your boyfriend?'

There is no boyfriend. Boyfriends are not part of your plan. You linger over the tartan Nessie draught-excluder, try on the tartan Scotch bonnets, marvel over the tartan toilet-brush holder, cuddly Highland bull with tartan grass, but finally go for the Tablet, both ginger and chocolate varieties.

'Come again,' says Jolly. 'Tell your friends we're always open, always ready. Twenty-four seven.'

The front garden has more gnomes than the Chelsea Flower Show, circa 1976, more gnomes than Gnome Heaven in the Caledonian Road, where all good gnomes go for a respray. It takes you half an hour to get down the garden path, what with the dinky little swings, wishing wells, the light aircraft for a gnome in a flying jacket, the three fishing gnomes on the three humps of a three-humped Nessie.

'Every year a new one,' says Jolly. 'On my husband's birthday. From his gran. They had a business together.'

You would ask her more – it sounds interesting – but it's stopped raining, mist is rising from the grass, and the hills are waiting. You take one last look at a gnome in a tutu on a trapeze, and set off along the track.

You walk all day, following a river upstream. By evening, you've done your fifteen miles and reached a high, fragrant meadow. You shake out the tent, fit the poles together, hook up the cover, peg out the fly.

You're sitting in the tent, surrounded by kit. Last Christmas, you told them exactly what you wanted. It had to be Karrimor, Berghaus, North Face. It had to be blue or green, no bright colours, that last bit for Mum's benefit. Mum will happily wear an orange T-shirt with a red hood, yellow trousers, pink belt, silver trainers. Dad, however, is strictly grey on grey. No wonder they split up. But they really did you proud, and it's not just clothing. There are Hurricane wrapround sunglasses, a silver whistle, Cyclone waterproof matches, a torch, compass, First Aid tin, even biodegradable toilet paper. (Thanks Dad.) And Kendal Mint Cake, which you eat – a square or two at first and then the whole lot because, after all, you've got the Tablet now; just as much survival benefit. Forget all that Ray Mears nonsense about stag-beetle soup, making yourself a three-piece suite out of split bamboo.

You're sitting in the tent with the wind flapping the sides, and you can't help remembering the three fishermen gnomes astride the three humps on the three-humped Nessie, then the whole tent fills with red pointy hats, shiny apple cheeks, idiot grins, and there's Jolly in her empty house. 'They had a business together,' she says. *Had* a business. Then it hits you. Not the business – the husband. In memoriam, a new gnome every year. They ought to have downcast eyes, folded hands, but they're unremittingly cheerful, so cheerful you have to pull on your boots and go and sit by the river.

'This is all that you need,' says the river. 'Bone, muscle, clean air.' And you know that it's right. Generations have walked these hills with nothing more than a pair of boots and something to put over their shoulders to keep off the rain.

Except that there's Dad, who has very little money, and Mum, who has even less money, agonising over every item, wanting you to have the best, and you think, in spite of what the river says, sometimes *stuff* is more important than anything: it's all that matters; all there is between you and the open beak of tomorrow.

In the morning, you pack everything then take your leave.

'Come again,' say the carved heads. 'Mind how you go.'

You stand for a long time, looking round, storing it up. Where the tent stood is a flattened imprint in the grass. Already, the grass is springing back.

Shush

▼

ON THE LAST SUNDAY in January we went out for the day, Sam and I. We went first to Tate Modern, going in through the great Turbine Hall, up the rough wooden stairs. On one of the middle floors we found an igloo made of slates and spaces and I couldn't decide if the spaces were to allow the voices of imagined inhabitants to escape or allow our voices to enter. Home is a curious thing, I thought. Especially nowadays.

'Too existential for me,' said Sam so we backtracked out of the building, reclaimed our car from the street where we'd left it, drove on, frost ferns still clinging to the corners of the windscreen. He was driving fast, our car an old thing covered with battle scars so that the other drivers gave way.

'They wouldn't have asked us over,' I said, 'if they didn't want to see us.'

But I knew he wasn't convinced – why would they want to see him? – it was all a fake and they were only being polite. Sometimes it was hard to keep going. I wanted to switch off, let things go.

We knocked on my daughter's door in Shepherd's Bush and, when she opened it, the baby was standing beside her, beaming up. 'Toy,' said the baby, running into the sitting room to fetch us one. Toy was a new word for the baby.

Her father wasn't there.

'Said to say sorry,' said Marina.

Apparently, he was working in an empty house in Hammersmith, stripping away layers of paint from eighteenth-century wooden panelling. I hoped he had a wireless on to keep him company then corrected myself '*radio*, not wireless,' then considered the proliferation of wires at home – extension plugs, eel-filled pools behind my chairs, wires and screens in every room, and remembered a birthday greeting that arrived last week courtesy of Yahoo, an e-mail cake with celebratory yellow icing that, transferred on to paper, became quietly tame.

We played with the baby while Marina cooked lunch. Later, after we'd eaten, I looked at her sitting in front of the fire, sagging into herself, her gold hair dull and flat, dragged away from her face, tied back. Work was stealing her energy. She had a new position as a manager and was still in the honeymoon three months, still the eager beaver in a world of new communication concepts, one in which change ruled, change on all levels, impulse and signal.

Upstairs, the baby was crying.

The crying went on undiminished for ten minutes then Marina said, 'The last thing I want is battles at bedtime.'

'Of course,' I said. 'Of course you don't.'

Privately, I thought the baby didn't want to sleep in case, when she woke up, Marina was gone. Mummy-gone-work was her first attempt at a sentence. It wasn't useful to criticise. Marina had made her choice and the baby would have to cope. Meanwhile, Marina sat looking distant, a little sulky. Worn out, I thought, and couldn't imagine being a career woman.

'You chose alternative, Mum,' she said once, when I was having a grumble. Strings of unsuitable men, unsuitable jobs. That's what *my* mother used to say – unsuitable being one of her words. Not that Sam was like that. He was simply the same as me, no real career, no real money, so we suited each other exactly. Anyway, there we were, my career-woman daughter drooping with tiredness and the baby crying in her cot.

'Let me have a try,' I said. 'Shall I?'

'If you want,' she said. 'You never know . . .'

That's right, I thought. You never do know. Maybe the baby will be so surprised at getting me when she wants you, she'll pack it in. Maybe I can still do something right. So I went up the stairs and into the back bedroom. The curtains were drawn and it was dark in there and I could only just make the baby out. She was standing in her cot, crying steadily. She watched me as I crossed the room towards her and I waited for the scream but, instead, she held up her arms. 'It's all right,' I said. 'Here we are – it's all right.' I braced myself for the struggle, but she slumped against my chest, going instantly into that bonded limpness where her head fitted sideways on to the shelf of my shoulder and I thought of her immaculate pink cheek, tear-streaked and soft, and hoped the thick fibres of my woollen jumper wouldn't prickle or scratch. She was still crying but now it was the dying tail-end of tears, the gulp and sniff of someone who has cried herself out but can't stop.

'Shush,' I said. 'Shush.' And went on repeating this, whispering into the dark, into her Johnson's baby smell, her waxy hair, into unseen shapes behind the wardrobe door, inexplicable folds in the curtain, the creep of encroaching dark.

'Shush.' Until, gradually, the crying stopped. I walked up and down the room, holding her close, not able to see if there were objects I might trip over, toys or clothes on the floor, taking small careful steps, rocking her, patting her back.

It seemed to work because now she was calm, maybe even asleep, but I felt, if I put her down, she would be up again instantly, probably worse than before, so I kept on walking and shushing until my arm was asleep. Against one wall was a sofa, one of those futon contrivances that are never comfortable, either as a sofa or a bed, so I edged myself on to it and she rolled quietly in my arms, her head slipping into the crook of my left elbow, her body sprawling across my lap. I looked down into her soft moon face, her eyes black and open. Her head felt heavier than before but there was no question of moving. Her eyes flicked shut then opened again. In the dark there were just these black smudges then the blank moon: smudges, moon; smudges, moon.

Earlier, she had danced at arm's length from the television, spinning and clapping, being a snake, a horse, a rabbit. She'd danced with a man in a suit that was almost Teletubby but not quite, a man, or maybe it was a woman (who could tell in that suit?), and a screenful of smiling children. They jumped and she jumped. They clapped and she clapped. *We* clapped and she spun round laughing. She loved it – this dancing in time with pixellated friends, this doing the wibble-wobble the Tumble-Tot way.

I listened to a television in the house next door and imagined Marina still on the rug by the fire, Sam on the big chair in the window bay, where I'd left them, and hoped they were having a good talk, not about the baby but about themselves, hoped that Marina had stopped listening out for the baby, was pleased it was quiet, was making the most of it. I was.

I was glad to be up there in the dark – the smudges, moon, breathing steady – glad to be connected with that abundance, that limitless world of openings in front of the baby. I wanted to stay there but felt them wondering about me downstairs so I rose and crept across the room then, inch by inch, lowered her into the cot. She blinked.

'Shush,' I said. 'Shush.'

My hand stayed where it was, on her chest, and I rocked her very slightly, stood there, bent over the cot, rocking her small body until my own body hurt, bent over like that, but she fell asleep again. I had done it. She had allowed me to put her to sleep. I was not as good as Mum but I was her granny and that was good enough.

Granny was not a name I was used to. The baby couldn't say it yet but my daughter had been using it for a year and a half. It sounded too old, too dusty. Granny was button-up boots, bedtime too early and boiled potatoes, never roast. It wasn't me.

But time had folded over me whether I liked it or not, labelled me neatly. Marina was Mum now but it felt just the same, this standing in the dark, this listening for the breathing to go slow. It was the same. The baby was one generation removed but it made no difference; we were the silk thread in the labyrinth and names had no meaning, the years between us had no meaning, the cock-ups, the walk-outs, the fights and struggles, all unimportant. The baby didn't know about all that – the past that always changes.

She was now and so was I.

I lifted up my hand and walked backwards across the room to the door, opened it, letting in the light from the landing, as little as I could, until there was enough space between the door and the frame for me to squeeze through, then I was out, negotiating the squeaky floorboards, tip-toeing down the stairs.

'Well done,' said Marina. 'That's brilliant.'

Her eyes said she didn't believe it, it was amazing, against all the odds, and the baby ought not to have settled without her. We looked at each other and acknowledged that but there was also gratitude, relief, and an understanding of her past and the baby's present overlapping.

'Not completely lost my touch,' I said, unable to help crowing a little.

'Obviously,' she said. 'Anyone for coffee?'

And while she was out in the kitchen, Sam and I looked at the Sunday papers that no one had opened yet.

'It's nice, isn't it?' he said.

'Very,' I said.

I knew Sam was thinking about the baby on his lap earlier and how she had turned over the pages as he read to her. 'More,' she said. He was thinking about the back of her neck and how it smelled and how there was still, occasion-ally, a hint of soreness in her creases, how new she was, her neck really being nothing more than a crease, and that newness being so important to him, that starting again. It was not about bloodlines, only the arms around you. Marina was his stepdaughter and the baby his stepgrandchild. He had no biological children of his own so they were as close as he got. Sometimes, they were so close he was rubbed raw and had to stand back. Sometimes they were so close, he dissolved. 'He's very intense,' said my mother, rigid with disapproval. Which was why I loved him. And I knew what he was thinking and he knew I knew, and we smiled at each other, then Marina brought in the coffee and I drank two cups even though it gives me stomach cramps.

The baby's father arrived, bringing with him the smell of freshly peeled wood and corrosives, Sam talked to Marina about his counsellor and how he was feeling better, and Marina said something about the importance of understanding that love wasn't finite, that if you gave some to one person it didn't mean there was nothing left for the next.

I listened to them talking and remembered the igloo. In front of its door, a line of jagged glass plates was clamped in place, one behind the other. At the end of the line was a spotlight but, even though it was switched on, the light rays couldn't penetrate all that glass. In the igloo, the pretend inhabitants had to live in hypothetical dark.

I imagined the threads joining us up, winding over this arm and that arm, running round a waist or a neck, spider thread running up the stairs and round the baby, round and round like a cocoon, round and round until the whole house was white with thread.

Windy City Man

▼

1

YOU'RE RIDING in a black cab across Rannoch Moor. You didn't even know they had black cabs in Scotland but here you are, hanging on to the back seat, the only car on the road as far as you can make out, which is not easy in this lot, the windows streaming, the driver steering through winds of up to eighty miles an hour. You love storms. Every time you come here, there's a storm or a flood. This time it's a faulty train engine as well, but the cab more than makes up for it – all the way from Glasgow Central to Fort William, ScotRail picking up the tab.

'On your own, hen?' said the driver when you climbed in. Hen? Like ducks, doll, lambkins, or *mon petit chou*. Eddie always calls Dad 'tiger'. In public. No way you'd put up with that.

Forget Eddie, forget Dad. Forget Mum. Forget the fact that Mum is now acting as if she's not Mum but some weird kind of flatmate, dance music on all the time – main mix, club mix, funky re-mix. Whatever happened to smooth jazz? Just before you left she went out and bought you a mobile. You hate mobiles. At college, you'll be talking to someone, batting an idea back and forth, then *bring-bring* and you're left to study your nails while they yammer on like Sibyl Fawlty – oh, I *know* – and the idea, which a moment before had seemed so important, so exciting, is brushed aside. It's hard to believe you allowed her to buy you one. 'For emergencies,' she said. 'It would make me feel better.' It might make her feel better but it makes you feel like a dog on a leash.

Forget it. Forget the lot of them. Here you are, on holiday, in a black cab in the middle of Rannoch Moor – the road floating over the peat like a plank at risk of being swallowed. In the end, you arrive in Fort William twenty minutes before the train you would have caught pulls in. It's still belting down and you're exhausted but you set off anyway, striding along until the lights of the town are completely extinguished, then you pitch the tent behind a dry stone wall and climb into your sleeping bag. It takes a while to warm up. It's April but there's still snow on the hills.

'Hi, it's me. Just ringing to see how you are.'

'I'm asleep.'

'It's only half past ten.' That's Mum, the night is young, let the party begin.

You tell her firmly that you'll be on the other side of the mountains tomorrow and reception will be out of the question. Then you ring Dad.

It's hard to picture where he is, having been to the new house only once and then it was nothing but unpacked boxes and ladders, a claw-foot bath in the living room, so you imagine him in a pizza joint – he likes Italian. These days he's also into flares, frills, sequins, satin. You keep telling him it makes him look older but he won't listen. 'What's wrong with happy?' he says.

'Hi, it's me.'

'Hello, sweetheart,' then, in an aside, 'It's Mira.' Why is it Eddie always has to get in on the act? Dad's hand must be over the phone because everything's gone muffled; Eddie's saying something. 'No, hang on,' Dad says, his voice clear again. 'Yes, later.' He must have taken his hand away. 'Where are you, sweetheart?'

'Fort William . . . yes, bed and breakfast . . . no, it's really good, chintzy, wood panelling, full English in the morning, can't wait . . . . yeah, vegetarian sausages.'

The next day, you're out on the track, the sky peeled bare by the wind. It's always different, always; the colours, light, cloud shadows altering the way you read the geometry. For five days, you head south.

On the sixth day, tramping beside a rain-shrouded Loch Lomond, cutting through forestry, you come to Rowchoish bothy. It's unlocked. They're always unlocked; that's the point – anyone can stay there. It's just like any other bothy, one big room, a few battered wooden chairs. It smells of smoke, not people, but they've left things behind: half a packet of soggy digestive biscuits, a washing line with clothes pegs stretching wall to wall, a yellowing copy of *Girlfriend in a Coma* by Douglas Coupland, and, in front of the hearth, a pile of dry logs and kindling. Why not make a fire? A fire would be wonderful.

Twenty minutes later you're sitting on one of the chairs, boots off, wet clothes drying on the line, flames leaping. You make a start on *Girlfriend in a Coma* but the next thing you know, it's falling off your lap, the fire has died down and you have to make a decision. This isn't what you planned. Still, where's the harm? Behind you is a raised concrete sleeping platform. All you need do is roll out your sleeping mat, get into your bag. You're stoking up the fire and thinking that you might just give Mum a ring in a minute, or Dad, touch base, when the door opens.

'This is cosy,' he says.

He's blocking the door, a long big-boned man who has somehow brought the forest in with him. All round the bothy, pine trees stand to attention. There are mosses, fungi, ferns, the shafts of light insufficient to break up the dusk, rather they deepen it, making everything charged.

'Hi,' you say. 'Is it still raining?' Which is stupid (water is pooling off him on to the floor) but you have the craziest feeling you've conjured him up somehow and you're trying to sort out what to do.

'Yeah, really coming down. Mind if I . . .?'

He looks at a chair and you smile. 'Sure, no, go ahead.' Be friendly, stay calm. This is what bothies are about – shared space.

'I'm Jerry,' he says, taking off his jacket, hanging it over the back of the chair. 'From Chicago, the windy city.'

'Mira.'

'Good to meet you, Mira,' he says, shaking your hand. 'Great city. You should go. Eighty degrees all summer, fantastic sandy beach. Frank Lloyd Wright's house. Ernest Hemingway's birthplace, great clubs, great culture.'

It's hard to get a hold on what he's saying. All the right gear, top-of-the-range trekking boots, just another walker glad to be out of the rain. Undoing his rucksack, he drags out parcels of bread, blue cheese, ham, tomatoes, sets it all out on the bench, then carves the bread with a pocket knife. He reminds you of Eddie, in his early thirties, all eager

beaver and boy scout, spoiling things, though not neces-
sarily through any fault of his own, but spoiling things
anyway, just by being there.

'And you?' he says. 'Where's home?'

The place you call home at the moment is a clapped-out
Victorian terrace house Mum bought shortly after Dad left,
a place she thought she was going to do up but somehow
didn't. Jerry is looking at you, one eyebrow up, so you give
him the Wobbly Bridge, the Tate Modern, but there's an
emptiness round your words that won't go away. You don't
care for buildings, new or otherwise, hardly ever go into
town. London is just a place where you live with Mum while
you get through college. London is not *home*.

He's smiling. 'Want some?' His arms, where his shirt-
sleeves are pushed up, are covered in red-brown hair.

'No thanks.'

'Go on, I've got plenty. It's okay,' he says. 'I've got a girlfriend in Dunbarton. Soon to be a father and soon to be
married. Everyone says, like, how it will change my life.
She's a bit crabby and I just want it to happen now. Last
taste of freedom. You?'

'Student.'

'Cool.'

'Not really,' you say then you're rabbiting on about defer-
ring your last essay and not being sure if you're on the right
course and how you thought coming up here might help you
make a decision.

'And has it?'

'Not yet.'

He's *exactly* like Eddie in that, before you know it, all this
stuff is spilling out, private stuff that you had no intention

of telling anyone and hadn't really thought about yourself.

'Sure you won't have something?' he says.

It seems rude not to and you're hungry so soon you're eating bread and cheese and he's picking up *Girlfriend in a Coma* and saying that's a great book, he read it years ago, can't remember it but it was great, really great, then you're swapping best places to stay and he's taking off his boots, telling you about the phantom bagpipe player on the slopes of Ben Nevis.

'Six-thirty a.m.,' he says. 'Woke us all up.'

'Us?'

'All of us at the campsite. All of us with massive hang-overs from the ceilidh the night before and this son of a bitch coming through the morning mist playing *Scotland the Brave*. Amazing.'

'How do you mean *phantom*?'

'Just this sound – this amazing blood-curdling sound, coming right past us, everyone with their head stuck out of their tents looking for someone to shout at. But not a soul. No one. Truly eerie.' He's taking a silver hip-flask out of his pocket, pouring something into a tin mug then passing it over, saying, 'Would madam care for a wee nip? Southern Comfort, nothing like it at the end of the day.'

And, just to be friendly, you accept. You don't drink; Christmas sherry, that's all. Oh, and nineteen vodkas on your nineteenth birthday. None since. This is strong but surprisingly pleasant so you let him pour you another and he has another and soon you're both talking, laughing and joking as if you've known each other for years, while the fire blazes and, outside, there is nothing but the black edge of the universe. You saw this when you went out to have a pee and fell over in the grass. You lay on your back getting soaked and where the stars should have been there was only space.

Later, when you know a great deal more about the windy city, Jerry takes his mat and sleeping bag, lays them down in a corner on the sleeping platform, gets in, and rolls over. You sit by the fire a little longer then, when you think he must be asleep, do the same, occupying the other corner.

Sometime in the small hours, you wake up. It's pitch black and he's standing over you. You're wide awake but can't see a thing. It's a dream, that's all – the heavy dark. You close your eyes, open them again, your heart jumping like a frog in a barrel. He's right there. You know he is; you can smell him – wet bark, resin. Don't move. How can you? Zipped in. His clothes rustle above you. What's he doing? Is he bending over? You can't breathe. Where is he? What does he want? You're asleep; he thinks you're asleep. Make yourself breathe. Keep breathing – slow, steady.

He stands there for a long time and you listen to your heart thump and think that it could have been the train driver falling asleep, a sheep dodging in front of the cab, could have been hypothermia or a rabid squirrel; could have been a crevasse or lightning. You have your new skates on and you're flying over the ice rink at the Sobell, flying towards Mum. 'Slow down, Mira! Slow down!' Mum is waiting to catch you but you're flying past and Mum is far behind now, arms outstretched, shrinking and shrinking, and you can't breathe any more. The ice crackles in your ears. You're waiting and waiting. Then the dark shifts and Jerry's gone. You hear him getting back into his sleeping bag, doing up the zip. You lie staring into the dark. Every now and then, a log sinks on the fire.

In the morning, he isn't there. His sleeping bag and mat are gone; his rucksack is gone. You get out of your bag, roll it up, pack everything as fast as you can, put on your jacket, hitch your rucksack on to your back. It feels twice as heavy as it normally does, your head hurts and there's a thump above your eyes. Stupid, it says. Stupid, stupid.

When you open the door, the sunshine is like needles, the grass silver with dew. There's the place where you lay down; there are Jerry's boot-prints on the wet track – arriving then leaving. You hate him then. Why did he have to spoil things? What did he want? You follow the prints round the side of the bothy until it's clear which way he's gone then turn round, start walking in the opposite direction. You walk as fast as you can but it doesn't seem quick enough.

Later, when you've calmed down, you sit on the side of a bridge, take out the mobile, press Dad's number. It rings once and your heart speeds up again. Where is he? It rings twice and you wait. You wait. The phone keeps on ringing.

'Hello?'

'Eddie? Hi, it's me.' It would be him, wouldn't it? Steady Eddie, Mr Always There When You Want Him. 'No, everything's fine. It's *fantastic*.'

'Your father's out,' he says. 'At an interview.' (Dad's an art teacher, unemployed because his school was closed down after failing its Ofsted.) 'He went for an interview last week,' he adds. 'But they asked him to teach history, geography and music – music, can you imagine?' You can't. Dad's like you – tone deaf. Eddie is still gabbling on. '"There's a syllabus," they said. "You don't have to make anything up." "That's

56

the problem," he said. Now he says he's never going to teach again. This interview – it's not a teaching job.'

'Oh?'

'Admin.'

There's a long silence.

'How are *you*?' he says.

So you tell Eddie how you camped at the foot of Ben Nevis and a phantom bagpipe player came out of the mists at six-thirty a.m. and woke you up. Absolutely incredible, like a regiment of pipers at the Edinburgh Tattoo. This *amazing* music, wailing, heart-stopping, skirling right past your tent. No one in sight. And you with a hangover from the ceilidh the night before. Drunk as a skunk.

'That's great,' he says.

Then you feel bad about lying. Like you've been tricked into it. You imagine him telling Dad and you remember all the other lies, some not worth remembering, some that won't go away. Like when you told Dad you hadn't been to college in months when in fact you went every day. Which is bad enough but then you imagine him ringing Mum and the whole thing entering into family folklore. Worse, there you are in the student union bar, 'There was this piper . . .'

Switching off the mobile, you put it away, hitch the ruck-sack on to your back and walk on. You have everything you need. Everything. You could go wherever you want, walk on for the rest of your life, in the world, really in it. Simply this, the click of stones under your boots, the passage of clouds.

▶

2

It's always harder going down than up. Your knees ache and your feet are sore. It doesn't matter how many socks you wear or how expensive your boots are, going downhill with a heavy rucksack is tough. A rescue helicopter clatters overhead towards Glen Coe. You've been lucky, not even a sprain or twisted ankle. You keep telling Mum, apart from the midges, there's nothing to worry about. You're not the only woman walking on her own; lots of women do it.

It's nearly dark but still warm, the air balmy, the track going down and down, across a stone bridge over a rocky gorge, through woodland, down and down, to enormous empty buildings, rusty sidings, gaping broken windows, concrete sluices and channels and, next to it all, a power station still supplying the grid. Kinlochleven, not the prettiest Highland village with its blocks of identical houses squatting at the head of the loch – houses, reservoir, aluminium-smelter, power station, all part of the same vast engineering project – and there, tucked between the river and the ruins, is a new bunkhouse and campsite.

'Just you?' says the proprietor, taking your money.

The field is crowded, as you'd expect in August, the usual cluster of geodesic domes, tunnels and suspension tents, leaving only one vacant slot – between the shower block and a yellow box tent with clear plastic windows, curtains and an extending floral canopy complete with matching floral sun-loungers. When you've pitched, you throw your ruck-sack inside, smear on some repellent (the river is bound to bring in the midges) zip up and set off for civilisation. Amazingly, the shop is still open and you nip in and buy a slab of Genoa cake and a ripe banana for breakfast.

Coming back, you see *that man*. Your heart goes into overdrive. He's walking over the grass towards the yellow tent. It is him, you know it is – the windy city man. Ducking into the shower block, you peer through the window. It can't be him. It is him. He's going into the yellow tent and your tent, rucksack, everything, is right there, beside it. Slipping out of the shower block, you run back round the corner, down the road, over the bridge and into the hotel.

It's noisy and cheery, full of walkers. You order a beer then take it over to a seat by the window where you can watch the door.

What if he comes in for a meal? There were two sun-loungers. He's brought his wife. Any minute now they could walk in. And what about the baby? Didn't he say she was pregnant? What was it he said – last taste of freedom? What are you going to do? You're going to have another beer and calm down. Your hair was long then; you were wearing different clothes. Look, you recognised *him*, didn't you? That isn't the point. Nothing happened, remember? Don't give me all that *he woke up in the night after a nightmare* rubbish, *he just wanted someone to talk to* rubbish. He's a creepy nutter and, seeing him again makes you realise that, for the last two years, he's been lurking at the back of your mind, waiting to pop out.

He didn't have the nerve, that was all. So what can he do now, when he's got his wife with him? Why wait to find out? You're going to go back, pack up the tent then walk on. He isn't worth it. It's late, it's dark, you're tired, you're surrounded by other people. What can he do? Nothing. That's all he did before, right? You're going to go back, get inside the tent, zip up and go to sleep.

It's nearly midnight when you return to the campsite; there are no lights on in the yellow tent.

In the morning, you hear them talking, Jerry and his wife. You grab your sponge bag and towel and head for the shower block. The shower doors are transparent. The water cuts in and out, too hot or too cold. You can't get the taps to turn and water runs all over the floor.

When you've finished, you head back towards the tent, intending to pack up as fast as you can and move on but they're arguing. Or rather she is; Jerry is pleading.

'It's like . . . it's like you're the big tiger and I'm a little bunny in the corner,' he says, 'and I'm scared. I don't like that, don't love you like I used to.'

'I fucked up big time then?' says his wife.

'It's like I said – you're so angry,' says Jerry. 'You never stop being angry and then I say stupid things. They just slip out because I'm scared. You fucking scare me.'

'Bullshit! You start stuff, mess up then turn it round on me.'

What does he mean, *he's* scared? What is she? A lady wrestler? Professional knife-thrower? This is just what you want to hear. You almost punch the air with your fist. Yes! Except you can't move in case you miss something.

There's a long silence then Jerry says, 'Why don't you just chill out?'

'You know,' she says, 'this is so boring; not you – I don't mean you – but this, this is boring. Arguing, all we ever do.'

'Right.'

'Yeah, right.'

There's the sound of the insect-screen being unzipped, a woman's hand emerges, then a foot in a blue trainer, a bare leg. You drop the towel and the sponge bag. You've forgotten to fill your water bottle. Grabbing it from under the tent flap, you walk briskly over to the tap on the corner of the shower block and turn it on, silver water pouring and twisting in a long rope, hitting the path, splashing over your feet. Jamming the bottle under the spout, you turn and look back.

A woman is coming towards you then going past, a large ginger-haired woman, pale creamy belly rolling over the top of her shorts, sunburned freckled breasts rolling under her vest. You want to tell her about Jerry, tell her what he's really like, but she's locked up in herself, tight ginger eyebrows, pale lashless eyes; shoulders up, she's past you now, striding towards a line of cars, getting into one, slamming the door then sitting on the front seat staring straight ahead at the road, as if it's the most interesting thing she's ever seen. A trail of perfume hangs in the air, Bodyshop, something light and floral.

In your pocket is a sprig of bog myrtle. If Bodyshop put that in a soap they'd make a fortune – Chanel No. 5 with a dash of cinnamon, a hint of black pepper. Last year, you sent Dad a letter with a sprig of bog myrtle tucked between the pages. 'The smell of Scotland,' you wrote. 'Forget fried Mars bars, forget Arbroath smokies and Aberdeen butteries, bog myrtle is the real thing – Rob Roy for Men.'

Why are you thinking about that now? In a minute Jerry will come out of the yellow tent and go over to the car. He'll go right past you. The water is splashing on your foot again.

The water bottle is full. You're reaching over to turn off the tap when the flap on the yellow tent opens and he comes out and starts walking towards you. He's distracted. He's going to go right past without seeing you and the words 'last straw' and 'camel's back' come to mind.

'Jerry, you shit!'

You put out your arm to stop him. You want to say more, tell him exactly what you think of him, but he turns towards you, his face puzzled. He doesn't recognise you, doesn't understand. He's wearing flip-flops and the grip on the soles must have worn away because he slips on the wet mud and goes backwards, one arm flying out. He's lying in water. The tap is still on. Reaching out, you turn it off.

'My head hurts,' he says. Afterwards, you're sure about that – 'My head hurts' – like a little boy then he shuts his eyes.

Someone has come out of the bunkhouse to help, someone runs over to the car to fetch his wife. It's not like before. In the bothy you were light-headed with trying to understand. You were angry – you hated him and why not? It was the first time you'd hated anyone; it took over and got in the way. This time you're calm and totally clear in your mind – there was no intention.

His wife comes running from the car, crouches in the mud and water, smoothes his hair. 'He can't be,' she sobs. 'He can't be. We're getting married next week.'

'I thought you *were* married.'

She thinking about Jerry and what's happening, that Jerry is what counts now, not some loopy woman butting in. Even so, she can't stop herself being polite. 'Jerry isn't married,' she says. 'Not yet. He's my fiancé.' And somehow this old-fashioned word, this *fiancé*, transforms her; you vanish and there is simply Jerry and she knows what to do. 'Jerry,' she whispers – 'Jerry . . .' then she leans down to kiss him, her hair swinging forward so their faces are hidden.

It happens then. You can't believe how quickly it happens. He sinks away inside himself, flattens down and grows smaller. It isn't something you've ever seen before. There's no theatrical twist of the head, no groan or gasp, simply this – this getting smaller. He's gone but your anger doesn't go; it's merely overlaid with new knowledge. He lies limply in her arms then the ambulance arrives and he's carried inside on a stretcher. She follows and you're left alone on the bench, in the sun, with everybody around you. You can't make out what they're saying – a hubbub, an uproar, but none of it comes through. You're thinking about how scared you felt, in the dark, waiting and waiting.

'He slipped,' you say. 'He slipped. It was an accident.' You sit on a bench in front of the bunkhouse, staring at a pot of bright blue flowers. 'He slipped.'

He slipped and cracked his head on the corner of the shower block. The rocks edging the path are painted white and one of them is marked with a drop of red blood. After a bit, you get up and wipe away the blood with your handkerchief then drop the handkerchief into a rubbish bin. The proprietor brings you a whisky but you pour it into the flowers when he's not looking.

The police arrive and ask questions. They ask everyone questions while you sit on the bench in the sun. They tell you to stay put until further notice. You've told them nothing about the time before. Why make a terrible situation even worse? You mooch round the campsite, watch the river crash down to the loch. You've been here too often in dreams, in crazy thoughts where Jerry gets what he deserves, but he didn't deserve this, did he? No one does. Taking your mobile out of your pocket, you tap in a few numbers then pause. You haven't told *anyone* what happened before, neither Mum, nor Dad, certainly not Eddie, not wanting to worry them. Why start now? Switching off the mobile, you put it back in your pocket, then, almost immediately, it rings. You can't get it to switch off; there's something wrong with it – ringing and ringing. Even when you hurl it into the river, it makes no difference; it's down there under the choppy water, ringing and ringing.

'No need for you to hang on any longer,' says the sergeant. 'We've got your details.'

So you pack up and set off, climbing up and up. All around you are the mountains and all of them have names, Gaelic names, English names, same pile of rock, different spellings, different sounds, maybe the same meaning – Rough Mountain, The Old Man, The Maiden. From up here, you can see the whole of the village, a new pier marching into the narrow loch, the old smelter, the new campsite and, right in the middle of the campsite, a bright yellow box.

Big in Japan

▼

RAY SEEMED ONLY JUST to touch it, barely a wiggle or a twist. The root was enormous, bloody. He slipped the tooth into his trouser pocket. Usually, the only thing he took with him on stage was a newly washed and ironed handkerchief – crisp, white, immaculate. What else would he have to put in his pocket? An eyeball, a finger? Oh God, was he going to have to go out there with his pockets stuffed with body parts? What was he doing? He couldn't do this, could he? There was no way he could go out there and sing. No one could expect him to sing like this, not even Leo Stunzel.

A root infection, the dentist had said, make an appointment at reception for next week. Next week! He wasn't going to make it through today. If only he had a few more hours. Maybe in the evening he'd feel better; the pain might be less. This was a nightclub, wasn't it? Brighton's oldest nightclub, so what was Stunzel doing opening at lunchtime? Sunday lunchtime is Jazz Time. Oh, yeah? It was always Jazz Time.

He ran a little cold water into the sink, bent his head under the tap, took a mouthful, rolled it over his gums (they hurt, oh God, they hurt), then spat it out. Pink. He lingered in front of the mirror running his fingers over new craters, working his tongue backwards and forwards, checking and double-checking. He hadn't eaten for three days. All of his front teeth had fallen out, upper and lower jaw. It was a plague, a punishment, the acid he'd taken years ago, drink, chewing gum. It was too many sweets in childhood – clove balls, mixed boilings. Would anyone know what a mixed boiling was now? God, he wished he didn't. It was Dundee cake on Sunday, treacle sponge on Friday.

Oh God, oh God, the back molar on the right was loose now. They were all going to come out, he knew it, and there was nothing anyone could do. He should have been out front an hour ago. What if he'd already died, not on stage but in life? What if this was an out-of-body experience, he'd come back into his own decomposing body and there was nothing left but corruption? He wished he *were* dead. When did he take the last painkiller? Two when he woke up, two with breakfast, two mid-morning, two half an hour ago. Putting his hands up to his face, he pressed the flesh over his jaw, willing it to keep his remaining teeth in place. The room moved away from him, grew dark, then caught him at the last moment, and he stepped through it, stepped out, and closed the door behind him.

Already the tables were crowded. Stunzel was casting him looks: get on with it. Ray walked to the piano. No one noticed but that was normal. He sat down and laid his hands on the keys. All round him the crowd went on talking, drinking, eating, waving their arms about, shouting, insulting each other, roaring with laughter. One or two had even gone to sleep. That molar was definitely loose. The tip of his tongue ferreted into a hole that wasn't there before. Try not to think about it.

He began to bring a little music into the room. He didn't have to sing, he could just play. Stunzel could go fuck himself . . . then there was one of those lulls, someone laughed a shade too hysterically, the heads turned, and Ray found himself singing. It was what he did after all. *Feelings* was his big number. No one could sing *Feelings* like he did but, today, there was nothing but air and sibilants. He was mumbling, whistling, his gums flooded with blood. He stopped singing. The punters on the nearest table watched him. He stopped playing. Blood continued to pour into his mouth. He took his handkerchief out of his pocket. The punters on the table behind the first table were watching now. Tentatively he withdrew the molar, put it into the centre of the handkerchief and wrapped it up, twisting the cloth tight, making it into a ball, then dabbed it at his mouth. Now everyone in the room was watching. Ray sat on the piano stool holding the blood soaked handkerchief to his mouth.

'Jesus,' squeaked a thin girl in gold-spangled trousers, 'Jesus!'

Over the top of the handkerchief, Ray could see Stunzel making his way across the room. Chairs scraped on the floor and a wave of diners recoiled as Stunzel strode towards him, a striped tie slithering on his chest, his face viperish. Ray didn't care. He was going home, he should never have come in.

'Get off,' Stunzel hissed, then raced past Ray to the console to put on the muzak.

During the following months Ray went repeatedly to the dentist.

'Problem sorted,' he told Stunzel.

Except it wasn't. The plate shifted when Ray didn't want it to, and interfered. He tried various adhesives, smearing the plastic roof with thick white glue before each perform-ance but it oozed round the sides, got under his tongue, so that his mind was hooked on it, waiting for it to happen – the boiled dog-bone taste overlaid but not fully disguised with mint, the seepage, the stuck-down feel, his tongue in the wrong place at the wrong time. He cut back his reper-toire and only sang requests and *Happy Birthday*. Then one Sunday Jazz Time, Stunzel appeared beside him again, tucked the tip of his tie between two buttons, rocked back on his Cuban heels.

'Not what I'm paying you for,' he said.

Ray turned and stalked out.

He went down to the sea, still wearing his penguin suit, his bow tie, crunching over wet pebbles, his shoes getting ruined, but what did that matter? He wouldn't be wearing them any more, not his patent leather. There was no one else on the beach, not even a solitary dog-walker. The February wind sliced across the shingle and he turned up his black satin collar and wondered if that smudge on the horizon was France or oncoming snow.

There was a new operation, a pioneering operation. The procedure involved two ready-made steel plates, the first being screwed into the jaw to support the second, into which the new teeth would be fixed. It was the only way he was ever going to be able to sing again, to feel confident enough to *really* sing. But six thousand pounds? Six *thousand* pounds.

He'd always lived day to day, cash in hand. He'd sung until his throat was sore, his voice a whisper, sung until his head swam in the mornings, all his energy burned away, but where had it got him? The only possible way to raise the money was to ask his daughters for a loan. Roz worked for the Law Society and Janice managed a leisure centre in Hove. Between them they could spare enough to cover his needs, surely?

But he couldn't possibly ask them and they wouldn't offer, which was entirely reasonable, neither of them knowing how his finances stood. He'd let them imagine he still got royalty cheques. Last week, he'd even told Janice that the band were still big in Japan. 'Great,' she said. 'That's great, Dad.' You didn't want your children worrying about *you*. You were supposed to worry about *them*. And he had, all the time. Especially after their mother died.

He stood where the barnacled legs of the West Pier sunk into the sea, where the current dragged and the shingle ground and shifted, where there was a drop of six foot or more, where you could slide under the cold until there was nothing but cold. He shivered, his white nylon shirt damp from the sea air, the ruffle squeaking in the wind then, picking up a stone, he tossed it into the surf, the seagulls bleated and someone scrambled over the ridge.

In a crowd she would have stood out, without one she was monumental, silver hair with the ends tipped purple, huge raw hands, outsize trainers, yet her features were delicate. A bright silk caftan slid over her generous body, fuchsia, carnation, violet, rose, a garden full of colours, so that she appeared to have been cast out of a time that went before, a time of incense and flowers.

Some women were like that, he thought, always trying to pretend it was summer.

'Look at that,' she said. 'Is it coming or going?'

A wafer-thin disc hung above the horizon and she began to sing, her voice deep and clear, rising and falling with easy precision. It was as if she'd stolen his voice: one moment he was dumb, Stunzel looming over him; the next she was throwing this song into the air.

Paper Moon, a happy-sad song he loved. Happy-sad were the best. Sad-happy another thing altogether. Nobody wanted those. It was as if she knew all about him, was mocking him. But that was crazy – only a musician would think like that, musicians and entertainers, all raging egos, children really. And clearly she wasn't like that; it was a gift, a wonderful no-strings-attached gift. She threw up her arms, wriggled her shoulders, the seagulls whirled, rainbow dazzles from a mirror-ball, and she could have been on stage.

Some people's lives, he thought, went steadily forward, security following on from early success. His was a collection of moments, islands arriving unexpectedly in fog. For months he'd been blindly floundering but now he was in the clear again. She was magnificent; her voice, his voice, it didn't matter; it was the song, tossed so casually over sea, wind, the sweep of winter sky, the song that was everything. She swung through both verses without faltering and then she was laughing and so was he, laughing on the cold beach and that astonished him. You had to keep going, no matter what – you went on. Fancy her knowing all the words, even doing the flourishes in between where you made your voice go growly and turned it into brass.

'It does look like paper,' she said and he thought how touching it was that she needed to say that.

'You've got a great voice,' he told her. He smiled at her, that is he made his eyes smile and pulled back the corners of his mouth while keeping his new teeth concealed. It was a smile that had taken practice.

'Do you think so?' she said.

It was irritating that she pretended not to know. Bending down, he picked up another stone and skimmed it towards the waves. It skipped twice then sank.

'Try this,' she said, offering him a round one with a hole through the middle.

'Won't work,' he said, but she threw it anyway.

He was thinking that there is nothing more preposterous than a middle-aged man trying to be playful. Worse – acting as if he knows everything. The stone skipped four, five, six, seven times.

She smiled and he fell into her smile, a cat into catnip, couldn't resist. Her purple hair stood up like a parrot's crest. 'You look frozen,' she said. 'Any special reason for the outfit?'

Let her imagine an all-nighter in a cream stucco mansion, he thought. Let her imagine dancing under a chandelier, satin sheets, a champagne breakfast. The nearest he got to that was the giant hardboard wineglass leaning tipsily from the roof of the club, reminding everyone that the place was once called Sparkles. Currently it was The Slammer and before that The Temple. It still boasted an Aztec frontage buried beneath a skim of chocolate-brown pebbledash, though the Paisley wallpaper in Stunzel's office belonged to a time when it was Club Noreik, as did all the other fittings.

'Party,' he lied. 'Last night.'

They strolled along the beach and he introduced himself and she told him her name was Jordan. 'Because my mother was staying on a kibbutz when I was born.' She told him that she lived nearby, came to the beach at least twice a week. 'Needed a bit of sea air,' she said. 'Clear the head.'

He didn't ask what might need clearing. She was about his age, somewhere between fifty and sixty and you didn't get that far without acquiring dross and sediment but not everyone wanted to talk about it. Sometimes he couldn't believe how much people talked. The band hadn't talked: they didn't need to; they had the music. Now the drummer ran a crystal shop in The Lanes and the others had simply vanished, not one of them having had the sense to sign the right bits of paper at the right time. Still, there was no point being bitter; that's what his daughters would say. No one to blame but himself. But he *was* bitter. He couldn't believe how bitter he was. How much had he got left? A rhetorical question; he knew exactly how much he'd got left – two crumpled tenners in his pocket, sixty-five pence in loose change.

'Coffee?' said Jordan.

'I know just the place,' he said, which he didn't, but it couldn't be hard to find. 'This way,' he offered, guiding her through a barrage of race-track traffic and up a side street and there, just as he was despairing, was exactly what he had in mind, a café with checked tablecloths, real flowers on each table, a bar at the back.

'You want to sit there? By the window?'

And she sat down on a straw-backed chair in the alcove, soft folds draping her legs, spilling over the mounds of her thighs. He ordered a cappuccino for her and a double espresso for himself then did his smile again. Whatever you like. Jordan looked across at the sweet trolley, hesitated.

'Go on,' he said. 'My treat.'

She chose a meringue – two snowy air-blown shells sandwiched with double cream and blood-red raspberries – ate carefully but, all the same, specks of meringue collected on the shelf of her enormous breasts. He allowed himself a little harmless speculation. Whatever scaffolding there was, it was lightly put together. She was taken up with the pleasures of sugar and cream, and he took pleasure in her enjoyment though he couldn't help thinking about his daughters.

There was no point really. None at all. They had their own lives and they'd made that abundantly clear. They'd gone suburban, moved into a class he didn't understand or care to understand, where you talked about the silver pepper pot you'd bought, the electric towel rail you were going to buy, the price of air travel. Ray didn't travel. He went from his flat to the club. En route, he passed everywhere he needed – corner shop, newsagent, launderette, off-licence.

'Yes,' they said, sinking their voices to indicate sympathy, nicely judged, neither mean nor excessive. 'Yes, that must be hard for you, Pops. I can imagine how you must feel.' Which was infuriating. How could they possibly imagine anything of the sort? He saw them holding the phone away from their ears as he talked, mouthing to their husbands – 'Dad – it's only Dad.'

He swallowed his coffee, pushed away his cup. He knew he wasn't a responsible parent. Children are supposed to ask their parents for help, not the other way round. He was nothing more than an old muso who'd let things slip, one of thousands. Brighton was full of old musos with fraying hair and no teeth.

Six thousand pounds.

'Brandy,' he said to the waitress. 'I'd like a brandy.' The waitress looked at Jordan. 'Two brandies,' he said.

Jordan leant back in her chair and lit a cigarette. Her eyes were enormous, dark-shadowed. She wanted too much; anyone could see that. She was one of those women who always want too much, too soon. He should get rid of her, move on.

'He was a lyricist,' she said.

'Sorry,' he said, 'miles away.'

She was talking about her father, telling Ray about the last time she'd seen him. Apparently, they'd gone to Ronnie Scott's when Ella Fitzgerald was on with Dizzy Gillespie. 'For days afterwards,' she said, 'I couldn't shake that song out of my head.'

'*Paper Moon*?' he asked, because she seemed to expect it.

She nodded. 'There were letters, phone calls, the visit at Christmas, then nothing.'

Now, Ray was telling her about his teeth, the club and Leo Stunzel. He went on and on and she talked some more about her dad and they both got drunk. At least, afterwards, that's how he remembered it – both of them talking at once.

'It was over a year before we found out he'd died. You wouldn't believe how much money there is,' she said. 'One song in the charts for thirteen weeks, eight weeks at number one. Don't ask me how many cover versions there are. And he wrote it for me – love song.'

She waved a piece of paper at him and for one wild, ecstatic moment he thought it was a cheque for six thousand pounds and he was back on stage, singing his heart out. Jordan was with him. They were singing a duet. Except that *actually* the cheque was nothing more than the bill. The waitress had left it on the table and Jordan had picked it up.

'Sit down,' said Jordan. 'It's okay.'

But he snatched the bill from her and rummaged in his pockets.

'Cheers,' she said, knocking back the last of her brandy. She couldn't stop talking. 'He died intestate,' she said. 'Can you imagine? All that money and the stupid bugger didn't have the sense to make a will. Heart attack. Never married my mother. I'm illegitimate. No legal claim. My half-brothers and sisters inherited and they're not going to acknowledge me now, are they – not in their interest, is it?'

He supposed not.

'Hope they burn in Hell,' she said.

That startled him. Her eyes were pink and the brandy had made her skin dilate and glisten. He caught a glimpse of himself in a mirror at the end of the room, corpse-faced. It gave him a fright. Sometimes you forgot how old you were and it hurt when you remembered.

'I meant to say,' said Jordan, 'thank you.'

'What for?'

'When I saw you,' she said, ' – the bow tie. He always wore a bow tie.'

Suddenly Ray couldn't care less what her father did or didn't do. He had things he had to do himself, things to sort out. Roz or Janice would be making supper soon and, if he hurried, he would get there in time. As for the money, all he had to do was ask. It was ridiculous. They loved him, of course they did; they wouldn't let him down.

He fished a card out of his breast pocket, one from years ago with gold deckle edges and a treble clef in the top right-hand corner, one from when the band still thought they were going places, the big time just around the corner.

'Any time,' he said, laying it on the table in front of her, bending over and giving her a kiss on the cheek.

'Maybe,' she said, 'we could . . .'

She was pillow-soft, creamy under her tropical dress, but the dog-bone taste was back in his mouth. What was she doing, taking tea with a scrap like him? He had the craziest idea. Maybe she was going to ask *him* for money. Why else would she have come up to him and started singing? All that stuff about her father – it was just a line. Going over to the counter, he settled up. Well, that was it, she wouldn't get anything out of him now; he was broke.

When he came back, she'd gone. His card was still on the table.

Picking up the vase of flowers, he threw it the length of the café. It flew over the tables, petals falling, light flashing off the glass, flew straight at the wall and shattered, the flowers sticking for a moment in a tangle of broken stalk and wet leaf, then sliding to the floor. One of the waitresses ran towards him, a mouthful of white teeth. Then there was Jordan, rooting about in a handbag, opening up a purse, making soothing noises to the waitress, taking out a note and laying it on the table. She'd only been to the ladies, it seemed, 'to powder my nose.' Hooking her arm through his, she steered him out into the street.

He didn't have any money; she didn't have any money; the whole world had money but not them; Janice and Roz, Jordan's half-brothers and sisters, Leo Stunzel, even the waitresses in the café, the skateboarders, day-trippers, foreign language students, pickpockets, joggers, they'd got it sorted: they understood the advantages of a secure financial life. Even the seagulls knew more about that than he did.

She hurried him downhill and, somehow, he managed to brush his sleeve over his eyes and collect himself. When they reached the railings on the front, she still had her arm hooked through his and he was grateful; it was a long time since he'd felt himself held by anyone. They stood in front of the ocean, side by side with their backs to the town, the dark expanding and opening up. He'd been below ground, he realised, and now he was coming up, like a mole into snow. The moon was no longer paper but heavy and round and hanging in front of them, solid as a gold record hanging on the wall of a sitting room they might once have shared. It ought to have made him sad but he was happy – happy-sad.

Gorilla

▼

SOMETIMES I'M STILL for hours. The longer I sit still, the more it pisses them off.

'He's not real, Mum. He's stuffed.'

'Course he's real. There, he moved.'

I'll slam myself at the bars in a minute and they'll scream. Show the teeth and they'll scream again. It was sitting still that first brought Garry over. He was a little guy, half-drowned in top hat and ringlets, pure bone wrapped up in striped silk and perched on six-inch hand-painted plat-forms. Not that you noticed the boots. It was the eyes that got you. Blue lightning eyes in a mud-coloured kisser.

'Wow, man,' he said. 'A monkey that meditates.'

I turned my head away slowly, turned my whole body away, inch by inch, quiet, calm, thoughtful, went to the back of my cage, picked up a handful of straw and shit, strolled back to the bars then hurled the lot straight in his face.

Garry didn't blink. Debris trickled off his hat.

'I bet you can levitate too,' he said.

He slipped me a Bounty. I undid it and handed him back the wrapper. If there's one thing I hate, it's untidiness.

Garry was the same, precise and unhurried, a creature of routine. Most days, he went to the rose garden and hung little silver-foil packets on the bushes, tucking them in under the blooms, then he sat down on the grass and waited for custom. He took the money off the punters then told them where to look.

'Check out the central bed,' he'd say. 'Yellow Rose of Sharon. Crimson Duchess.'

Usually, he dropped a little something into my drink.

'Stay loose, man,' he said.

Garry was the space between people, the side-step into the dark.

He sat on the grass lounging and smoking, and one by one the needy would come and go. He brought a tranny and turned up the volume so it made a room of sound, a secret space no one entered without permission.

'Come in, man,' he'd say. 'Got a light?'

He was the king of dreams but I was your nightmare. All the big stars came to see me. Everyone. They wanted that buzz. I was Kafka's beetle and God saying No! I was Harry Lime watering down penicillin. I was Hiroshima and Dr Mengele. Pop stars, royals, journalists, they all came. Oh yes, I was in the Sundays. 'A Life In The Day Of'. Bloody nerve. All that stuff about Lomie. You don't know about Lomie? You've forgotten? Lomie was supposed to be my mate, soulmate. The public wanted a baby gorilla, something cute to ooh and aah at. Just the thought made me shudder but I didn't have a say, it was all decided.

'Lomie arrives next week,' said my keeper. 'Bet you can't wait. Twenty and still a virgin.'

I gave him one of my looks, showed him my teeth, may even have banged the bars a little, I don't remember. Put it this way, I wasn't amused.

Garry understood.

'Why get upset, man? Like sex is everything? What do they know?'

Just the same, twenty years is a long time to live on your own and I had bachelor habits, the whole pad to myself, empty space.

'No such thing as empty space, man,' said Garry. 'Not even a cage. All space comes pre-packaged, filled with dreams.'

Garry could say what he liked and I didn't mind.

We used to do the clubs together. He had an arrangement with my keeper, a regular supply in exchange for the key. Garry needed protection and that was where I came in. Of course I was also a marker. Spot the gorilla and you were home. In Soho, we used to head down an alleyway, slide down the stairs to the basement and knock on the door. Bang in the middle was a peep-hole with a shutter. The doorman opened it up a chink. He was built like me, long arms, barrel chest, wide as the door.

'How many are you?' he growled. 'Oh hi, Garry, how ya doing?' Then to me, 'Hi, man, nice suit.'

Before I went out with Garry, I'd spend hours getting ready, sitting in my den and combing my hair. Garry was just as fastidious about his appearance but he liked you to think his clothes were an accident.

'Why think about things, man? Just let them happen.'

I wished I had some of his cool. I was edgy, thinking about Lomie and what she might expect. It was only days before her arrival and I was beginning to lose it. The sun hurt my eyes during the day and at night I couldn't remember where I was. The clubs were all the same, dark and cobwebbed. The coloured lights spun on the ceiling but the walls were roughcast concrete, the floors stank of urine, the girls of patchouli, the steps of vomit, the doormen of Brut.

Garry fed me downers.

'When in doubt,' he said, 'go with the paranoia. Trust me.'

I ran up the bars and swung from the ceiling.

'Forget her,' said Garry. 'Last night of freedom, right?'

We baby boomers were never logical.

I made myself presentable and waited in my den. It was nearly midnight when I heard Garry talking to my keeper.

'There you go, man,' he said. 'Be happy.'

A moment later, the back door opened and Garry smiled, all brown teeth and gaps. I used to get through thirty ice-cream cartons a day and as many sweets as I liked, so I was particular about my teeth. Not Garry. Smiling was a mistake. Like a chasm opening up, the sudden drop into the dark.

We strolled through the park, cut down into Camden Town, then up West. Nights had a pattern we didn't like to vary, party-hopping in Belgravia, clubbing in St James's, run-ins with the local fuzz, run-ins with the local heavies. And girls. Always girls. They told Garry he had a cute bum, which he did but he never took things further. Girls were good for business, decoy ducks, but Garry and I were a double act. He let them buy us a drink though. Vodka and lime was my tipple. Rum and black was Garry's. Lomie never drank anything but milk. Two pints a day. Disgusting.

Forget Lomie. She hadn't arrived yet and the night was still young. Some time in the small hours we were back in Regent's Park, by the rose garden. Garry took a packet off a bush, sat down on the grass, opened it and rolled himself a joint.

'My grandmother was a Salishan Indian,' he said. 'A long time ago, man, when the world was young, there were only a few stars in the sky. Now they are countless.'

Here, he paused, inhaled slowly as if he were smoking a peace pipe, narrowed his eyes and leant forward. He leant so far forward, I thought he would fall on his nose.

'Each star is a campfire, man. Where the spirits can warm themselves.'

He meant people spirits. We animals were meant to stand in the cold and the dark and watch. Garry could be a bit of a jerk at times. Most people have only four grand-parents. With Garry, I lost count. In addition to the Salishan grandmother, there was also the last gypsy to be hung for horse-stealing, the first woman submariner, a Chinese herbalist, a polar explorer, a Russian violinist, and an African princess brought to Liverpool by white slavers. The last I could believe. Garry had a short nose, wide mouth and silky brown skin. He also had a Liverpool accent. Some-times.

I lay back on the grass and imagined I was shopping with Garry, buying a suit in Lord John, pin stripes and a bowler hat. I bought a cane with the stars of the zodiac inlaid in ivory and a silver tobacco tin.

'Your grandmother is a Micmac Indian,' said Garry. 'And your grandaddy was white trash. You came out of the Cali-fornian dust bowl and you live in LA.'

I gave Garry a hug. All right, so three hours is a long hug and I was seven foot wider than Garry but there was no need for him to freak.

'Far out,' he said, closing his eyes.

I looked at him lying on the grass. All over his waistcoat were hand-threaded beads. His buttonhole held an orchid. It always did. I put out my hand and touched his cheek but he didn't stir. It struck me that he might get cold so I went over to the roses, pulled off the petals and heaped them over him. I stripped most of the bushes before I got him covered. My hands are tough and I didn't notice the thorns. He looked peaceful. As if all the gaps in the storm clouds had closed up and now there was only rain. The lightning in his eyes had gone away, flashing off into the distance.

'See ya later,' I said and took myself home.

The next day my keeper announced the new rule. No Feeding The Animals. No sweets, no ice-cream. For three days, I stayed in my den, lay on the floor, moaned from time to time, and refused to move. Nothing happened. My keeper ignored me. He looked pretty rough in fact and every now and then he moaned himself. Eventually I got bored, went out into my show cage and took up the lotus position.

My keeper looked as bad as I felt. Sweat stood out on his brow, his hands shook.

'This is terrible, man,' he said.

I gave him a look.

There was a kid on the other side of the bars with a triple-decker Neapolitan, an easy snatch, but my keeper didn't notice.

'Got any Valium?'

What was the matter with the guy and where was Garry? The space on the grass was empty, not so much empty as empty of Garry. A couple with a baby had put down a blanket and the girl was making daisy-chains. She slipped one over the baby's head and laughed and suddenly I felt sick. There should have been music, Garry's beautiful room and the hungry stepping sideways through the sounds. There should have been Garry. I closed my eyes.

'He's not real, Mum.'

'Yes he is.'

'Don't he look like Dad?'

I threw myself at the bars, beat my chest and hollered. The little kid's ice-cream fell to the ground and he burst into tears.

'Now look what you've done,' said his mum. 'You big bully.'

The next day, Lomie arrived.

'Hello, darling,' she said.

I ignored her and waited for Garry but he never came. My head was still full of light and sounds and I groped around for my Coopers pellets, scratching in the straw. Like, I ask you, why do they have to throw them on the floor? Lomie kept diving in, snatching them up, laughing at me and jumping away. Last thing I felt like was playing silly buggers.

With Lomie, I lost heart. Not that there's anything wrong with her, don't get me wrong. Lomie is a nice chick, if a bit of a hayseed. What got to me was the way she messed things up – banana skins, cabbage leaves. I like to stow the left-overs in my bowl but she just tosses them over her shoulder. It's little things like that that can sour a relationship. I mean she doesn't even clean her teeth. They're brown like Garry's. Every time she grins at me, I want to punch her in the face.

I did once or twice, we even had a wrestle, but I couldn't pretend to be interested. Lomie was a drag. Whenever I looked at her, I felt ashamed. Like I was letting her down. Crap. I never asked her to move in. Didn't fancy her, that was all. As I said, she's a great kid really and it wasn't her fault.

After a while they took her down to Bristol where she had a fling with Sampson, her dreamboat she called him. Leaky skiff if you ask me, all bilge and no boiler room. She came back and had her baby. I insisted on separate sleeping arrangements after that. I mean a guy has his pride. She does her thing and I do mine. Now, I never go out. I stay in my den and let Lomie entertain the crowd.

I sit with my back to them and think about Garry, think about the last time I saw him, the way he lay down after I'd hugged him, lay on the grass and looked up at the sky.

'It's all in the mind, man,' he says. 'All in the mind.'

For Guy the Gorilla 1946–1978

The Student

▼

CHRISTOPHER HAS a special dispensation for being late, his tutor having accepted that this condition is better not pried into and might, if left unchallenged, gradually disappear. Christopher hates being late. He flies in, scarf ends flapping, coat falling off his shoulders, 'Sorry, so *very* sorry, thank you . . .' hoping, as he sinks into a seat, that his fellow students will imagine him running from the station then up the stairs. It takes him a further half-hour to settle and, until he does, he can't make sense of what anyone says. Smiling, he leans forward as if paying close attention. This tutor is better than previous ones. The last one was at him as soon as he came through the door. If she'd had X-ray eyes she would have seen him hovering on the other side, his hand reaching for the handle then falling back again.

Today he follows a new strategy – leave early, walk around the vicinity, allow himself to be distracted. He jumps off the tube a stop before his usual one, cuts through Russell Square and across the road. Up ahead a group of women block the pavement – dry cleaning, dry sherry, Chanel No. 5. Individually they're probably charming but collectively they bring to mind all those times he's been buttonholed at parties. *'And what do you do in Life, Christopher?'*

It's years since he did anything in Life. Once he worked in the office of his uncle's factory on the Great West Road, a factory turning out fancy silver furniture for wedding cakes. Once, though he finds this hard to believe now, he played lead guitar with a band. After that, there were shops, forecourts, pubs, a stint putting spectacle frames together and then . . . well, it's hard to remember, hard to figure out. Life is not something he wants to consider, not now when he's trying to get himself to class on time.

He brushes long black hair away from his face, squeezes his scarf tighter round his throat, and strides past high railings. This is better. He used to come here from school. St Francis Catholic School for Boys was very keen on this place. Every year, they shunted their boys through its corridors, a treat Christopher looked forward to – the mummies, the rock crystal skull, ferocious magic on casual display. He hurries in; there is still at least an hour to kill.

But where there used to be a shabby closed-off courtyard with the dome of the old Reading Room in its centre, he finds a huge glazed-over space, the Reading Room newly encased in a sparkling white stone skin. Twin flights of stairs wind round it. You can almost hear the harps, not to mention a celestial choir in full voice, but Christopher, who is no longer religious, imagines a roof garden with a fountain. Maybe he's been watching too many gardening programmes. He can't resist gardening programmes, *loves* them. Only yesterday he bought himself a bunch of scarlet silk poppies from a pound shop, compensation for the slush and draggle of December.

Setting off up the right-hand flight, he runs his hands over the chamfered edges, lets his fingertips trail along the groove in the parapet until they're coated with white dust. He can't help stopping to stare at the stretch of glass above his head, warm cobalt at the edge, coolest ultramarine in the middle. At the top, there's a barricade – *Restaurant Closed* – but just as he's turning away, he spots a side passage and a door.

'Allow me.'

Flashes of gold light fly off the flat planes of the stranger's spectacles.

'Thank you,' says Christopher, seeing the crowd in the room ahead, thinking that this is not at all where he wants to be. 'Thank you.'

It's darker inside the room, like shade under trees. Edging in, he begins to circulate. Imagine going up an escalator and suddenly noticing that, on the opposite escalator, every second or third person is someone you recognise. You don't know what to say. 'Hi,' you start. 'Hello.' Then peter out. There's the little Egyptian with lapis lazuli eyes who looks as if she's just stepped out of a spaceship, Chairman Mao with his right hand raised in salute, the discus thrower (well they would have him, wouldn't they?), a seated Buddha, and Tara with her elongated ears, high round breasts, narrow waist. What's so odd is finding them together. Usually they're segregated – Romans in the Roman gallery, Greeks in the Greek, and so on, never higgledy-piggledy like this.

One at a time, thinks Christopher. You're asked to have a group conversation but you have to introduce yourself first. That's how it is with groups – names first. At least that's how they do it at the Institute. The ice-breaker. Go round one at a time. 'How are you, good to see you again.'

Then go round and ask, 'How does it feel to be here together? working collectively for the first time? because I'm assuming this is a first for you. For me. You're used to being in groups but you haven't been in *this* group before, have you?'

Although geography and chronology have been disposed of, categories haven't. Somehow Christopher isn't surprised. *Abstraction, Drapery, Perfection, Guardians.* He doesn't know where to start. *Others?* A little to the left of Venus is the big Nigerian, the one with black-and-white markings, filed teeth and raised facial scarring, his favourite Nigerian, but now he sees there's something uncomfortable in the way the hands are held out, palms up; the eyes are impassive but the hands say sorry.

'You wear your heart on your sleeve,' said his lover. 'It puts people off.'

'I'm not talking about *people*,' he said. 'I'm talking about my mum and dad, my sisters for God's sake, brothers. I'm talking about you!'

And there he is slamming his fist at the wall, making a hole when he only wanted a gesture, a ragged black hole in a wall that turns out to be plasterboard.

'Jesus!' she said. 'That is *it*. Oh, Jesus Christ!'

'It's only a wall,' he said. 'What does it matter?'

There he is kneeling on the floor, crying and spreading Polyfilla, watching the grey sludge turn slowly white. It's rough and lumpy, needs sanding, but at least it's filled again, the hole hidden.

'You might say sorry,' she said, just before she left.

Now he lowers himself on to a bench, wedges his bag between his feet. There is an eight-line poem in the bag, iambic, trochaic, seventeen copies, one for the tutor, one for himself, fifteen for the other students. His heart hammers. He will have to go in a moment. He's too hot, a slow burn in his head, top lip sweaty, inside of his elbows, backs of his knees.

The worst thing is knowing, with absolute certainty, no two ways about it, that the homework which he has laboured over all week is worthless trite rubbish, pretentious nonsense. What was he thinking about? In half an hour he will have to hit the streets and by then it will be dark. The other students will be pouring towards the college, would-be actors or computer-programmers, those wishing to manage their anger, reach their inner child or touch their toes. He will have to squeeze through them all. He will have to get there on time. It's hopeless. He might as well go home now.

Except he can't. No matter how difficult it is, he must go to his class. He's firm on that. Only by going can it get any easier and can he turn things round. It's too late for Life but personal satisfaction, artistic achievement – those are still on the agenda. He has to believe that but, meanwhile, here he is in a room full of ethnographic plunder with the lights dimmed. If he could just remember some of the other students' names. There's a woman he likes – they went for a drink together – but he can't remember her name. It's ridiculous. After eight weeks he still can't remember her name.

Slumped on the bench, he listens to the controlled thud of the doors as newcomers file in and out. There are two doors, one on either side of the room and he sits between them. He doesn't want to be here, not with all these people tiptoeing over the carpet. Are they all killing time? They remind him of the heron on Finsbury Park lake, on the lookout but too well-fed to care. Tourists with bags, schoolkids with mobiles, the bored and the amazed, a young girl in a tinsel crown and a lavender fleece. Why are they whispering? As if any of these guys would mind – the dead shaman prepared for burial, the Hindu goddess without her head.

Do not touch. Even the lightest touch damages the exhibits. But looking isn't enough. Never mind the implied expectation that it is, or should be, that the sculptor or the subject is somehow staring out of blank eye-sockets, that you have only to look hard enough to communicate. Who's to stop him and what real harm would it do? Christopher has a dim memory of being shouted at once before. *'Hands off, laddie!'* But there's only one warden, half asleep at the far end of the room. Keeping his face blank, Christopher stands up, strolls past the tattooed woman with her protuberant stomach, past a rain-giver from Jamaica, past the big Nigerian again. Adrenalin rushes round his body. Inside his jacket pockets, his hands are prickling. Which one? He goes round twice before he comes to a decision.

Prince Khaemwaset is carved out of ordinary sandstone conglomerate. He's Egyptian, over three thousand years old and beginning to crumble, his polished surface interrupted, his chest cracked open, revealing water-worn pebbles, fragments of pre-existing rocks bonded in alluvial cement.

The pragmatic Christopher says, 'This is crazy. What can possibly happen?' The superstitious Christopher tells him to stand back. Stand well back. He steps closer, stretches out his hand. His hand trembles. What does he expect? – a twist of stellar energy? To be burnt, or frozen? Will Prince Khaemwaset speak to him in a spectral voice? *The End of the World is Nigh, nuclear dark descends tomorrow, asteroids, insect plagues, cloned zombies, the curse of the Mummy's Tomb, I am the God of Hell-fire!* But it's just as he thought. He touches Prince Khaemwaset's innards and no lightning comes to strike him down; there is no voice, only a calm emptiness he takes as a gift.

When he slips into the classroom, he's forty minutes late, the tutor has given her usual talk and the room is brighter than usual.

'Now,' says the tutor, 'homework. Did everyone do the exercise?'

Christopher smiles and leans forward.

She begins to go round the class, each student handing out their copies then reading their work aloud, in turn.

'Christopher?' she says.

He takes a single piece of paper from his bag, coughs.

'Sorry, no copies.' Coughs again. 'My chest . . .'

'Take your time,' says the tutor.

He gives a final cough, pats his chest, clears his throat, then reads aloud.

'Carved in air . . .' he begins.

The poem is not iambic, not trochaic. It has no rhymes and the syntax is a mess. Listening to himself read, he thinks it's not even a poem. It's about finding yourself alone and not knowing any more how to be with people, not knowing if you can trust them, not knowing who you are, when everything you say or think, everything you feel, is wrong. Stupid, thinks Christopher, reading on. Why didn't you go with the original? I haven't done what I was meant to, they'll either laugh at me or ignore me. But when he finishes, they clap. They don't usually clap. In fact he can't remember them clapping before and the woman he likes is smiling at him.

He's almost certainly blushing. He watches them talking about his poem but can't hear them, back in that time when all he did was cry, when anything could set him off, a hungry child on TV, two words left off a postcard – a bare signature instead of 'love from'.

He sits there thinking that enough time has passed to put half a self together, that half a self is better than no self and not to be sniffed at. They're looking at him, smiling.

'Would anyone like to go for a drink?' he blurts.

'I would,' says the tutor. 'After class.'

He drinks bitter shandy with Bella-Marie. That's her name. The others are there too but he's squeezed up in a corner with Bella-Marie, the woman he likes, and all he can think about is the way her tongue comes out and licks stray froth off her upper lip, the way her hair slithers over her eyes. She's wearing leggings under her skirt because she's been to Dance Impro first. He tells her about the white dome and Prince Khaemwaset.

'Did you know,' she says (his heart sinks at this; it always sinks when anyone says this, dive-bombs to the permafrost floor). 'Did you know that conglomerate was high-status stone, difficult to work with, therefore extra prestigious?'

It turns out she took Religion in Ancient Egypt last year and Hieroglyphs the year before. Christopher hauls himself back up to the light. It's good, isn't it, that they share an interest?

Later, he escorts her to Holborn tube then walks on to Liverpool Road, where he lives. Some of the street lights are missing and you can see the stars. He can't remember the names of the constellations and he's standing staring up at one that could be the Plough but might be Orion when he's jostled against a wall. A man goes through his pockets, takes his wallet. Christopher is sure that the Plough has seven stars. The hands go through his pockets while he counts.

'Give me your bag,' says the man.

After he's gone, Christopher can't remember what he looked like, only that he wore a baseball hat. He's a little annoyed about his bag and his wallet but he isn't frightened. Maybe he will be later. The main thing is he still has this afternoon's poem, in his head. He recites it to the drunks and stray dogs, to the rough-sleepers, to anyone who passes, to the empty street, his front door, the fading glow-stars on the ceiling above his bed.

La Luna

▼

TOMORROW WE'RE GOING to Macy's and I'm going to buy something on every floor. Already we're holding hands, snuffing up the warm sweet air like lions catching a long-forgotten scent. We stand on the corner of Herald Square, taking it all in, then follow the map to the hotel. It's a good hotel but not grand: a canopy over the street so you can make it from the cab without getting wet, but no doorman; a certain amount of marble in the lobby but no real opulence. A compromise that suits us both.

'Credit card, sir.'

Rick opens his wallet, hands one over, and we wait while the desk clerk taps into the computer. There is that moment as always, that clutch at the heart, but everything checks out and we take the lift to the fourteenth. In Las Vegas, the hotel was topped by a neon cowboy whirling a rope of stars; in Miami it was simply brash, in Savannah colonial. In between, we roughed it: trailer parks, empty summer shacks, easy-to-break-into long-abandoned farmhouses high in the Appalachians. In one place, in a cupboard, we found a .22 rifle. I took a photo of Rick standing on the porch with the gun in his hand.

'Don't smile,' I said. 'Scowl.'

Pulling the hip-flask out of my pocket, I take a swallow. In this room there are sachets of coffee by the coffee machine; a shower that works; body lotion, shampoo, cakes of Pears soap, thick white towels; and a wide bed you could make love on all night long, a bed we negotiate like honeymooners, nervously laying out our clothes, sitting on its edge.

The last bed back home was four-poster pine, first twelve months free, no deposit. They've probably taken it already. And the telly, and the sofa, and the rest. I can't remember how many homes we've set up. Suddenly I think of the house in Bristol, us going off quietly one morning as if we were just going shopping, the garden full of freezers and fridges jam-packed with frozen crab-meat, scampi, lobsters, octopus, a lash-up of wires trailing across the lawn, the whole garden humming.

There are musicians in the next room. They practise for an hour – saxophone and penny whistle – then go out. Thoughtfully arranged on the table-top is a subway map and a magazine full of restaurant reviews. I leaf through the magazine while Rick's in the bathroom. Down below the wind churns through deep stone canyons, past the cast-iron buildings, the Chrysler and the Flat Iron. Sirens. I can't keep away from the window. Light slips over the big buildings, fish over rocks. It makes me happy. There's nothing worse than wind blowing through trees.

'You hungry?'

Rick has showered and his hair lies slicked against his head. His skull goes down flat at the back to his neck. My father's head was dolichocephalic, a bean sticking out on a pin. He used to cycle to the pub, his head gliding smoothly above the hedges. Three heads wins the lady a china clown.

Rick is looking at me, impatient.

'Ravenous,' I tell him.

He opens his wallet again, pulls out the credit card, lays it on the palm of his hand, and wiggles it so the little hologram eagle flies.

'Three more days. If we're careful. Ready?'

'Ready.'

When we set out, his wallet was fat with cards, a flock of eagles. Now there's only one. I say nothing about the three days, though it comes as a surprise. I want to tell him, I love you. He strokes my hair. Last time we had sex, I curled into his side and told him I adored him. Funny old-fashioned word.

'I don't want to be adored,' he said.

Quite right, but just the same it hurt. My father used to brush out of the house while my mother stood there, eyes full of tears. 'Your coat,' she'd say. 'Your coat.'

He'd slam down the hill without it, the weight of her love hanging in the house, muffling me into a silence I couldn't break.

'Indian?' Rick says. 'Thai? Greek?'

'Italian.'

La Luna lies at the south end of Mulberry Street, where Little Italy merges with Chinatown, where the jewellers' shops glow with trinkets: frogs, dogs, rats, a dinky golden car, easily transportable wealth, one step up from having your teeth filled with gold. 'Never sell,' said my mother. 'Always pawn.'

La Luna is just past Umberto's Clam House. 'Where,' I tell Rick, quoting from the magazine and pointing at the bullet holes in the window frame, 'Joe "Crazy Joey" Gallo was shot dead in 1979.'

Rick doesn't respond.

Beside the doors, there's a plastic Bambi half-hidden by a barrel of daffodils. I give it a pat on the head. Last year we raised fifteen thousand pounds with a start-up business loan from Leicester City Council when Leicester was City of the Environment. Recycled plastic to be turned into fence-posts. I wasn't sorry to leave Leicester, wasn't sorry to leave Bristol, but leaving the last house was a downer. I'd almost got to know the neighbours. Rick ruffles the daffodils.

'Sure you won't change your mind?'

We'd had a tiff on the subway. Rick wanting something grander, me saying I'd rather stretch it and have the three days. La Luna has no bullet holes, no flowers, only a shrivelled artichoke on a plate in the window, a heap of tagliatelle the colour of Hoover dust. Honest and unassuming, the review said.

'A dump,' says Rick.

Instantly, I'm depressed, my shoulders stiffen with effort. The whole street looks tacky. Taking a quick swig from my flask, I think: this could be the last time you do this. But that's stupid. There's always going to be restaurants with Rick. In the Camden house we didn't even have a cooker.

Rick holds out his hand and I pass the flask over. He tips his head right up, takes a long drink, then gives it back.

'After you.'

La Luna appears to be the same as it was when it first started out, the benches battered, the tables rickety, the mural along one wall cracked and peeling. I can't imagine why I insisted on coming here. All this continuity and looking back, it drives me nuts.

'Australian?' croaks the waitress from smoke-charred lungs.

'London.'

'Ah, London. You gotta spotted dick? My niece, come back from England, said she ate spotted dick. You eat spotted dick?'

'Not all the time,' says Rick. He's wittier than me. When I make a joke it's not expected and can pass unnoticed, my puns seem accidental, my *double entendres* mistakes.

'It's good?' says the waitress.

Her face beneath the heavy make-up is too old to be pretty. Forty, I think, coming up for forty; a little bitter with it all, sad and angry under the smile. No way am I going to be working when I'm old.

'Very good,' says Rick, smiling back.

'You wanna sit here?' She shows us to a table right at the back in a room off the main room.

'I'd rather be at the front.'

'Here's quiet.'

'I don't want quiet. I want to be with the action.'

'You want action?' says the proprietor, butting in and taking over. 'You talk to her,' indicating the waitress. 'She's action.'

He beckons us to a table inside the main room, clears away the remains of someone else's meal, exchanges the soiled cloth for a pristine white one, then waves us into seats which rock a little on the uneven cement floor. He looks round for the waitress. Shouts. 'Maria!'

She brings over two glasses of water, sets them down; two plates, cutlery, napkins, a loaf of French bread, a bottle of olive oil.

'You lucky people,' he says, handing us a menu.

We choose while he waits.

'That it?'

He disappears and returns almost immediately. His look, as he lowers the carafe on to the table, is both condescending and battle-weary. He makes a tired movement with his hand that says 'Help yourself.' His trousers are torn and the top button on his fly is undone, his neck dotted with black moles.

Rick pours the wine and, just before he drinks, I stretch out my glass to his and we clink. I'm not superstitious. I can walk under ladders, but there are some things I don't care to miss out. Breaking off a piece of bread. I dunk it in oil.

'D'you know, I've never had oysters.'

'Oysters? They weren't on the menu.'

'I know, just saying.'

Near us, in a broken frame, is a blow-up copy of a testimonial from the Governor of Maine. All over the walls are photographs: starlets and comedians behind cracked glass. At the top end of the room, by the window, a big group is celebrating. Their laughter rolls back to us, edgy and abrasive. 'My mother was in the dream,' says our neighbour. 'Mother, flames, death, birth, blood.'

I take a big gulp of wine and immediately it lifts me up.

The proprietor returns with our salad. As he moves away, I notice the stitching has come undone on the back seam of his trouser seat. A little white shirt tail sticks out. 'Are the luckiest people in the world,' he sings, gravelling his voice like Satchmo's.

'*Il Patrone*,' says Rick, not knowing Italian, only guessing.

We eat strips of aubergine marinated in garlic and salt and get quickly drunk.

'I'll sort something out when we get back,' Rick says. 'I will, I mean it.' He reaches across and takes my hand. 'That's a promise.' I believe him and don't believe him, a trick I learned a long while ago; how to hold two opposites in my heart at the same time. Sometimes it makes me tired; sometimes it makes me quiet.

Il Patrone comes back and I wonder if he can see in our faces all the things that haven't worked out, wonder if he's thinking: another pair of losers, another pair of jerks. He whips the cutlery off our plates and lays it on the tablecloth again, lining it up as if it has never been used; then takes away our plates and comes back with two bowls of spaghetti drowned in thick crimson sauce. Rick's has slices of fried mushroom on top, otherwise they're identical. He places a jar of grated parmesan in front of us, showers black pepper over our bowls.

'You lucky, lucky people,' he says, then sighs and moves away between the other diners.

Maria stands at the back of the room, watching him in that unseeing way that tells me they are man and wife. Her legs are slender and her feet slipped into small tight shoes. Her toenails will be varnished tomato-sauce crimson and he will put his big freckled hands on her legs, slide them up over her shin-bones, over her knees, and her eyes will be very distant, and his will be soft and wet. His hands will be clumsy.

'You wanna big one?' He's talking to two young women. 'You gotta big one.' They giggle. Moments later something large, long and drowned in the same crimson sauce arrives. 'Big one,' he says. 'Enjoy.' This time, as he goes by, there is white flour on his trousers.

When the bill comes. Rick lays the card on the saucer and I watch Maria whisk it away. The name on this one is J. M. Bird. Rick signed it back in London and I remember wondering if J. M. Bird was Janice or Julian.

When we come out, the trees are lit up with fairy lights. The other restaurants have flowers on the tables, glitzy mirrors, cane chairs, waiters in crisp uniforms giving us the hard sell as we pass along.

'Hey, Frank,' yells a heavy blonde woman, lowering herself into a black stretch limo. 'Hey, Frank, we shopped, we ate. Take me home, baby.'

'Hey, Rick,' I whisper. 'Take me home, baby.'

He smiles and holds my hand and we walk down the road, everything temporarily forgotten, smoothed out and put away.

In the hotel we can do what we want, no dead parents on the mantelpiece, no unsold merchandise in the hall, no bills, no recorded delivery. We take off our clothes and climb into bed, switch on the telly, lie back on the stiff white pillows and kiss. The bed is solid and silent.

Afterwards I say, 'That was the best sex I've ever had.'

It wasn't. I just said it because I wanted it to be. He doesn't believe me, though it was good. He flicks the remote, channel-hopping, I'm almost asleep. Suddenly he drops the remote on the floor, rolls over and wraps himself round me, his cheek rough against the nape of my neck, his hand on my breast.

'It won't always be like this,' he says.

'I know.'

Sometime in the small hours I wake. Rick is standing by the bare window, looking out. There ought to be moonlight, but the light changes colours: neon pink, orange, green. He's naked and I prop myself up on one elbow and prise my eyes open.

'What is it?'

He doesn't answer, only pulls the curtain shut.

'Rick?'

'On the subway – ' he says. 'Woke up just now and remembered a bloke on the subway – '

I can only just make him out. He's picked up his jacket and he holds it for a moment like a mother with a dead baby, then throws it at me.

'Bastard's lifted my fucking wallet,' he says. 'Cleaned us right out.'

I sit up and go through the pockets. He's having a nightmare: this is not really happening. Now I'm in the nightmare. *Il Patrone* is in the room, and Maria. His face is lugubrious but hers is downright malicious. He takes her in his arms and they waltz round the room. 'Are the luckiest people in the world,' they sing.

Picking up my pillow, I bury myself beneath it, but their voices come through. From now on, every pillow I sleep on will have them inside, mashed into the feathers like dust mites, a chorus in my ear.

I sit up again, swing my legs off the bed and go over to

the window, throw the curtain wide. Now there is moon-light, high above the towers, a thin crescent moon. Rick's face is pallid. I grab his hand, half expect it to be cold.

'We can't let them win.'

'No?' he says.

'We still have our passports, our tickets.'

'Don't – '

'Don't what?'

'Don't say: and we still have each other.'

I let his hand drop and he turns and looks out of the window. The middle of the night and fourteen floors below there are people and cars. There is no night, only dark round the edges.

Lost Boys

▼

'AT HOME,' said the invitation, nothing formal. I wasn't a social animal, hated parties, but the weeks, months even, had been sliding by, and I knew if I didn't go I'd only end up bitching to all and sundry about the state of my love-life – non-existent state of my love-life – and that would have made me a sad bastard; another sad bastard to add to the collection at work.

I work for a local authority, relocating difficult children from school to special unit then back again to school. It may sound like *Catcher in the Rye* but it isn't really. You fall into stuff and that's how it was with me, the Job Centre sending me for an interview and me thinking No Danger, then getting taken on. Local authorities are repositories for all the saddos.

However, it wasn't work I was thinking about that morning. I stood in front of the long cupboard in my bedroom like a murderer staring into a drain through which had passed the boiled and strained remains of a decade's corpses, a murderer who can't imagine how he came to be like this, no longer remembers when it started and can't imagine when it will end. But, before you skip on to something more cheerful, bear in mind that I only said *like*. *Like* a murderer. It was just a feeling.

Inside my cupboard were hundreds of white cardboard shoe-boxes and I was tempted to take one down, open it up, check that the contents were still as I remembered, but the secret of successful design (whatever you may hear to the contrary), the *real* secret is no self-referral, no retrospection, no nostalgia. Each shoe was a one-off, worn for one night and one night only. Hence the feeling.

Rabbit shoes, fruit-basket shoes, rhino shoes with horns, cavalier, cowboy, sharks, even bed-of-nail shoes. I rummaged through my fabric box, pulling out tassles and Chinese patterned silks, snakeskin, pony-skin, half-heartedly debating the possibilities of postage stamps, even padlocks, but decided, after a day of it, that fetish was better left to Vivienne Westwood. I didn't go to art school all those years just to do platforms. Ah, I hear you say, what's he doing working for a local authority if he trained to be an artist? And this is where I put you straight. Virtually everyone employed by a local authority is trained to do something else. That's what I meant about repositories.

The radio bleated from a shelf. Apparently it was St David's Day.

On St David's Day, my grandmother, my Welsh grandmother, Blodwen Anastasia Todd (they had proper names in those days), always wore a daffodil in her buttonhole, never once forgot. It might have been spring but it wasn't a daffodil spring. Cold enough for snow. Forget daffs – too Mother's Day, too Easter Bunny. But Blodwen winked at me from her grave on the side of a bare Welsh hill and, in a flurry of inspiration, I sketched a design in the margin of a library book. I have no compunction about drawing in margins or adding notes, or inscriptions for that matter.

Reading an annotated book is as good as holding hands.

I hunted through various greengrocers' for the largest leeks with the longest roots. They had to be fresh and firm. They had to be deep Hooker's green on the outside, sweet yellow lime on the inside, a fat white stump at the base. I bought four to allow for prototypes (past experience says that you never, ever succeed the first time) then hunted for the right base shoes, size nine stilettos, any colour. Tried Oxfam, tried Romanian Orphans and was finally successful in Cancer Relief. They were even comfortable.

I walked them up and down while the ladies behind the counter smirked. Of course I played up to them. Who wouldn't? I can do theatrical, I can do camp, though I'd rather not do eccentric. Tucked away beneath my clean boy image, the crisp white shirt, grey flannels, my poor mad mother stares at the telly, in love with a newscaster, and Blodwen is coming through the back door to rescue me, though it felt more like kidnapping at the time. If only they knew, I thought, but I wasn't being fair. Both ladies had a distinctly In-Love-with-a-Newscaster look themselves. They had glazed eyes, fragile hair and they smelt like Mother – dried roses and Vaseline Intensive Care.

Back home, I sliced the first leek lengthwise to within an inch of its base, cut out the heart then slipped the left shoe between the leaves, pushed the pointed toe down into the stump, glued the outer leaves along the sides. Superglue is wonderful stuff. I over-lapped and bunched the leaves at the back. It was tricky but a little perseverance and I had it. Then I sheared off the leaves with my sharp cook's knife, wrapped a pale inside leaf up the heel, let it fan out a little at the back. I was careful to arrange the leaves at different angles, to lay the dark against the light until the shoe appeared to be made entirely from vegetable, a bulb-toed pump with a curly root flourish.

Sitting down, I tried it on, crossed my legs, let it swing in the air. Perfect. I got up and put Etta James on and, while she was giving her all, *I'd rather go blind* and *Don't pick me for a fool*, I made another to match, varnished them both, then knocked up a quiche with the remaining leeks and two eggs. I didn't have any cream. Which annoyed me.

The following evening, I ran the clippers over my hair, put on my grey Italian suit, my best suit, sixties mohair, newly back from the cleaner's. For a few hours, I'd be sharp as a razor blade. That was the theory. I slipped into a pair of white silk socks – yes, I know, Essex boy, but no other colour would have worked with the leeks – then I put on the shoes and stared into the mirror.

I wasn't young any more but I wasn't old. The mirror confirmed this. Neither one thing nor the other, in between, neither charmingly innocent, nor innocently charming.

All this effort and now, predictably, I was down. Call it stage fright, call it what you like; it makes no difference. Everything had to be perfect; everything *was* perfect. Except for my ears – huge, jutting, pinkly translucent, snail trails of light on the rims. And why did I only have one eyebrow, joined in the middle like a transmogrifying werewolf? I turned the mirror to the magnifying side, plucked out the hairs with my tweezers until the space between my brows was an angry pink. I couldn't possibly go. Even as I decided this, I picked up the phone and called a mini-cab.

Purse, spectacles, keys. The spectacles are five years old with round goofy lenses. I don't really need them, yet if I go out without them some dipstick is bound to wave a British Rail timetable at me, or a phone book, never a book of love poems or photographs of interesting people looking fabulous. It took forever to find the keys, turning over the heaps and welter, the underside of previous creations, snippets of pink suede, drifts of feathers. When I was at school the teacher used to say, 'Nigel, a tidy desk is a tidy mind.' I never understood the advantage of a tidy mind. All the same, I couldn't help wondering why I didn't have a special place for my keys, a brass plate on a whatnot in the hall. Maybe when I'm forty . . .

When the cab came, I sat in the back; there's nothing like inhaling the musk of other people's dreams, watching the city reel by. London is the best city in the world and I should know because I've lived here all my adult life, have never lived in another city, unless you count Birmingham and that, well, frankly, that isn't a city any more than McDonald's is a restaurant.

Birmingham was where I took my degree, where I made my first pair of shoes – crocodiles with real teeth from a shop behind New Street Station, second-hand teeth that leered at me from green baize plinths in the window, drawing me in. I had to have them. The next morning I woke with someone else's stomach curled against my back, someone else's arm heavy over my ribs.

It wasn't a reassuring door – a battered hulk, driftwood peeled from a shoreline, traces of paint clinging like salt. Behind me, the alleyway faded into the dark and, above me, there were balconies, hooks, relics, mysterious chunks of rusty metal embedded in brick, horrible dangerous things that could have dropped down on my head at any second. Maybe they wouldn't open the door. It was the wrong night, or the wrong door. Maybe, just maybe, there would be someone I hadn't met before – a possible. I was sweaty-palmed, dry-mouthed, all the usual symptoms. I should have taken a Valium. Get on with it, I thought. Ring the bell.

'Come in, come in, thought you weren't going to make it.'

'So did I.'

'Yeah?'

'Trains,' I said vaguely then sprung up the metal stairs behind my host, the leeks going up as if they'd dedicated their life to climbing stairs.

I wondered if they'd know how to come down, if the root toes would trip me up, if I'd have to turn and lower myself backwards on all fours like my sister's baby Aimee, ten months, who just that week had learned to go upstairs and then down, Aimee who held up her arms and crinkled her eyes in a smile that I believed was especially for me even though it was more logical to suppose she was only practising and smiled like that at everyone.

When we went in, I saw at once that the room was full of rich bastards or people who spent their lives making people richer than them even richer – total schmucks. Couldn't imagine why I'd been invited. I edged into a room full of flat-edged smiles, slipstreamed myself into the shoal. Big fish, little fish. I could always get loaded, I thought. Later, if all else fails.

'Darling!'

'Lovely to see you.'

'Darling, your shoes! How fabulous! Look everyone – Nigel's feet. Why haven't you got a shop, darling? Somewhere delicious where we can come and buy delicious things?'

Obviously the leeks were a mistake. I gave a little wave, pretending to spot someone I knew, clumped across the room, and buried myself in a suitably bucolic corner, flowerpots with grasses, the sort of thing that suggests a pent and suicidal moggy who, in between running up curtains and shredding wallpaper, chokes down dusty blades and stalks in the hope of making itself sick, a cat that is never allowed out. After a bit the grass triggered off the hay fever so I had to decamp, this time opting for a sky-blue leather sofa next to a table covered with huge glass bowls brimming with raspberries, strawberries and blood-red sangria. I spooned down some raspberries and began to cheer up. Was there, could there be, in all this smooth-jowled agitation, a possible?

It was late but no one seemed to be drinking – the kind of party where everyone has a breakfast meeting in a few hours' time and can't afford to drink. Filling a glass, I sat back, swung one leg over the other, let the sangria seep into my brain. The toes of my shoes were bluntly, sweetly fleshy. I am yours, I thought, to no one in particular.

I had another glass, and another, then there by the window I saw someone and between us the smiles darted, the current flowed, and I put up my hand, stroked my cat's fur scalp, rubbed it the wrong way. It was a long time since anyone other than Aimee had rubbed my fur, the wrong way or *any* way. Uncrossing my legs, I stretched them out, pointed the shoes directly across the room, smiled a long slow smile: I am not a little fish, I am your little fish.

'What wonderful shoes.'

'Yes,' I said. 'I like a little frivolity at the feet.'

When I got home the next day, it smelt like a tenement out of *Nineteen Eighty-Four*, cabbage soup, dirty underwear, but it was only the leek trimmings, wilting in a trapezoid of sunlight on the floor. My shoes were pinching my toes. Taking them off, I carried them barefoot across the room. The white socks were still under his sheets at the foot of a bed I hadn't cared to explore, not since the time I'd encountered a slimy knucklebone buried by *that* possible's dog, a border collie with a tongue it couldn't keep to itself.

I opened my cupboard and looked at the boxes, remembering the smell of wet hair after a shower, a birthmark the size of a rose-petal pressed on to an upturned buttock, remembering . . . well, remembering too many details. The process of seduction these days is like doing a job interview, each of you explaining the intricacies of jobs neither of you is interested in. Leek Shoes worked in the Westminster Reference Library, not that I let that faze me. As I said, it had been weeks, even months; besides, it gave us something in common. One local government officer to another, even helped speed things along.

Reaching up, I opened an empty box, dropped in the shoes then sat down on the bed. If I find myself sinking, it's a habit of mine to think about a polar bear. The bear dances on sheets of ice, pirouettes, graceful, powerful. Sometimes the bear skates on two legs, head up, front legs held clasped behind its back. Sometimes it glides on one leg. That day, it reminded me of school.

We used to slide on a strip of ice that formed each year in the yard, at the corner of the kitchen block, where the guttering dripped, used to stand in a long line waiting our turn. Strangely, the big boys didn't always go first, ice making them charitable, the little boys venturing out with wing-stick arms as if the air could catch them. Where were they now? No doubt leading useful lives but lost – lost to me. Here the bear returned, plodding in a tartan overcoat on all fours like a manicured poodle taken for a walk, trudging over white snow under a white sky. After a bit, all I could see was the tartan coat.

I changed into jeans and trainers, caught the tube to Oxford Circus and John Lewis and, for once, went straight past haberdashery. In the children's department on the fourth floor I bought a pair of gold kid slippers with T-bar straps, tiny gold buttons, the neatest buttonholes. I undid them then did them up again – neither too tight, nor too loose. They sat on the palm of my hand and I stroked them with my thumb, the softest leather you could buy. Made in Italy. Size one.

'Gift-wrapped,' I told the assistant, then wrote on the card: to Aimee with love. Big kiss.

Outside, Oxford Street was dark with impending rain. Men and boys floated by, dangerous animals. I watched their shoulder blades beneath their jackets, long legs cutting through the tide. For some reason, I thought of Blodwen sending me off in the mornings, smoothing down my hair.

Fourteen and her still tucking in my tie. 'Beautiful you are,' she said. 'Break their hearts, laddo, break a leg.' Used to make me cringe.

When I got home, there was a message on the answerphone.

'Thanks for a lovely time. See you tonight. Dinner at Yamina's. I'll pick you up at eight.'

Yamina's was the new Moroccan on the corner. I'd been meaning to try it. What I couldn't figure out was how he'd got my number and how he knew where I lived. I played his message over again, then again. He had a deep voice, a warm smiling kind of voice and I had the strangest feeling I'd been thrown a line and it would be churlish to throw it back. Stupid even. Etta James was still on the player so I pressed the play button, *Only time will tell*, then opened my cupboard and looked at the boxes.

Several years ago, I'd made a pair of yellow Moroccan mules with silk embroidery and curled-up toes. It took me a few moments to locate them.

Launch Party

▼

JANICE LEFT in November, protesting that something had been rubbed out along the way. At night the sky was filled with fireworks as if the population, enraged by the endless round of terrorist bombing, had let loose a fire-hail of their own. Harry went to Highbury Fields and stood on a mild night watching explosions behind the black branched trees. The moon hung in the sky, providing a sense of permanence while everything else collided in streamers of light. Banks of speakers relayed *Carmina Burana* at full blast, and he cried, tears leaking and rolling over his unshaved face. He stood in the crowd, his head back like a child's. Da da da da. The drums vibrating in his stomach, the massed choir. He could have wet himself. Da da da da. Then it was over and the lost children were being directed to the St John Ambulance and the flames from the bonfire reared up behind him, children in neon collars waved sparklers, people danced. He went quickly home and every firework after that, flaring behind his curtains, was an affront, a reminder of how easy it was to flip out of control.

Harry knew he should change his job and move away, buy a new flat, but he didn't. He went on sitting at his desk in the library. The public came in waves, as they had for the last twenty-six years, lapping up to the counter and retreating; sometimes a big splash, but mostly just little ripples nibbling away at him.

He directed someone to the advice centre, found someone else a copy of the *Which?* guide to vacuum cleaners, then went for lunch. Dog tired. The staff room was chilly and unloved, staff chewing Mars bars and flicking through the pages of *Hello!*. He gulped cold ratatouille made the night before then went down the back stairs to the basement.

Chamber after chamber, as dark and secret as a Pharaoh's tomb. He switched on the lights and began to walk between the stacks. A combination of computerisation and chronic understaffing meant that the basement reserve stock was uncatalogued and unretrievable in any practical sense. Harry had heard the Head of Libraries talking to the Neighbourhood Librarian.

'We're looking into ways of getting rid. It's not a question of selling. The books are too far gone.'

Harry saw seagulls wheeling over tips, shrieking in grey skies, a mulch of pages thickening and compressing into detritus. The Head of Libraries had once been a member of the Socialist Workers' Party, stalking round the library in denim dungarees and workmen's boots. Now he wore subtle suits with loud ties and his cheeks were smooth and jowled with sixty thousand pounds a year. The king of jargon. 'Let me bounce that past you.' 'Let's put that one in the net.' Little phrases he hid behind, camouflaging cuts and redundancies.

Harry paced past the stacks, past the mayor's chair, past a row of open-toed men's sandals (God knows what they were doing there), boxes of decaying children's stock – ideologically unsound volumes cleared out in the purges, Kipling, Blyton, Potter – past rusty buckets and raffia waste-bins, fire extinguishers, two vast tables you could dance on, roll-top desks, and a fly-blown collection of popular prints that people once borrowed for their living rooms. On and on and on . . .

And here it got heart-breaking – shelf after shelf – books from all the libraries they'd closed down, books pulled off the shelves because they didn't go out often enough, books that were sticky and grimy and falling apart, books that were simply old; leather and embossed spines stamped with Dewey numbers and, after them, rows and rows of the old Browne system.

Up above they'd say, 'Have you seen Harry?' but no one really cared, no one would look for him, not in the basement. There was supposed to be a ghost, the little flower-seller, a whiff of lavender passed down into staff lore. Harry didn't believe in ghosts, but he thought of himself as a psychic explorer, feeling his way into layers of accumulated memory, walking step by step into a collective experience that no one cared to share, no one could share because no one really knew it existed.

Reaching up to the shelves, he took down a book and it sat in his hand like a bird that was dying. Rough matt black, the colour flaking off the spine so that the raw linen and card showed through. Top and bottom, a row of tiny gold stars alternating with crosses. After a moment, Harry realised that the top row was actually letters, condensed fat letters that read like stars.

✶ G E N E S I S ✶

Inside, thick creamy leaf, covered with library marks:

Reserve Stock stamped no less than seven times, a green gummed-in label – Reference Library – in pretentious fiddly lettering, and in biro, scrawled in capitals and underlined twice, REF ONLY DO NOT LOAN, a square of brown paper glued over another label, pencil scribble, numbers. Sheer vandalism, graffiti; that's all it was. All that marking and stamping, totally over the top . . .

He turned the first page, noting the uncut edges, the thick ridged weight of the paper, the rearing unicorn watermark that leapt straight into his heart. Title page: GENESIS in dense black letters, lamp black. TWELVE WOODCUTS BY PAUL NASH WITH THE FIRST CHAPTER OF GENESIS IN THE AUTHORIZED VERSION * THE NONESUCH PRESS SOHO MCMXXIV.

Once Janice had shown him a book of engravings done between the wars. 'Nash was the best,' she said. 'Not perhaps technically, but pure magic.'

Another four Reserve Stock stamps in smudgy ink and the letters CPL pierced out in dots with a punch. Central Public Library, twice. More scribble, more biro rampaging backwards and forwards, outdated numbers. 'Look what they've done,' he whispered as if Janice were there beside him. 'Look what they've done.' Another stamp, violet ink, the Dewey number 761.2 NAS, a stock control number and, underneath, in hard grey pencil handwriting, Book Auction Records 1980–81. £240.

Someone had been planning to sell it after all.

Over the page in bold black letters: THE EDITION IS LIMITED TO THREE HUNDRED AND SEVENTY-FIVE COPIES * THE CUTS ARE PRINTED FROM THE WOOD AND THE TEXT IN RUDOLF KOCH'S NEULAND TYPE

ON ZANDERS HANDMADE PAPER BY THE CURWEN
PRESS FOR THE NONESUCH PRESS * THIS IS NUMBER
72. And on into the book.

It was as if the bird in his hand had opened its eyes and
sung with its very last breath. He was laden with guilt,
someone who had stood by for years watching the slaughter
and now, suddenly, understood.

He looked at the first print, a black oblong with two
worn-away corners, a delicate erosion of the dark: IN THE
BEGINNING, his eyes stroking the page. The next with
lines floating horizontally, light hitting the edge of a wave,
two thicker lines coming down, a curtain drawing back:
AND DARKNESS WAS ON THE FACE OF THE DEEP AND
THE SPIRIT OF GOD MOVED UPON THE FACE OF THE
WATER.

It made him feel lonely. There he was, down in the
bowels, as forgotten as the books, while, up above, they were
bleeping away on their new technology, scurrying about
saying, 'No, I'm sorry. It doesn't seem to be in stock.' Of
course it bloody wasn't. It was down there with him. He
looked up from the page and glanced around. The other
books faded into the dark like a queue waiting for welfare.

He looked back at the book and the lines became planes
that drew into curves, dancing, bending columns, then
peaks and valleys. AND GOD SAID LET THE WATERS
UNDER THE HEAVEN BE GATHERED TOGETHER
UNTO ONE PLACE AND LET THE DRY LAND APPEAR.

It wasn't as if he was religious, he'd given that up with
childhood, but the book breathed passion; a combination of
faith, craft and love that was meant to be shared.

Then looming, wearing a mask face hinting at Africa,

came the animals, AND EVERYTHING THAT CREEPETH UPON THE EARTH, a man and a woman side by side, described in Cubist planes that were limbs and not limbs, buoyant and sombre, containing a warning and a declaration and a newness that did not know hope because it had not yet been defeated.

Harry slipped the book under his jacket, went quickly upstairs and concealed it in his briefcase. All day it burned into him, the seagulls jeered, and a hand clamped down on his shoulder. He took it home and looked at it again, suddenly rose, went into the bathroom, brushed his teeth, ran a bath. Janice's toothbrush was still in the mug with his own. He soaked himself for over an hour without washing then pulled the plug, dried himself, and spent the rest of the evening in front of the television. In the morning he took the book back.

A week later he brought it home again. As an afterthought, he added a little blue book that caught his eye – *Science and the Common Understanding* by J. Robert Oppenheimer. The BBC Reith Lectures 1953. Oxford University Press. Amen Press, London EC4. Again the biro, violet stamps, punch marks, cancelled catalogue stamps, numbers that no longer had any meanings. And on page 11, in quotes, a passage by Isaac Newton:

'It seems probable to me, that God in the Beginning form'd Matter in solid, massy, hard, impenetrable, moveable Particles, of such Sizes and Figures, and with such other Properties, and in such Proportions to Space, as most conduced to the End for which he form'd them . . .'

Although he took the book at random, Harry saw at once

it was connected to the other, that they were all connected. From then on, he smuggled books home in his briefcase, nightly loads that began to accumulate in his flat, tower blocks of escapees sprouting over his carpet. He arranged them alphabetically in strict Dewey order, some from each category, not chosen with any real plan but by instinct because, like most librarians, he knew very little about books, not enough to tell the precious from the cheap. To him they were all precious. He cleaned them with surgical spirit and a soft cloth, and pasted in the loose leaves.

He dreamt about being found out. What if he were ill, if someone should carry him back home unconscious, and open his front door with the key from his jacket pocket? There was the Head of Libraries solemnly picking up a book and reading aloud the words REF ONLY DO NOT LOAN. Words like summons, tribunal and resignation began to thunder through his head, intruding into the trivia of filing and time-sheets, the endless in-putting of joining forms and the compilation of loan statistics.

The solution came to him one evening as he was going home on the tube. He had the heart of the library stacked on his sitting-room floor, its soul. The rest, mouldering and dusty, was disposable, skin and flesh rotting away in the ossuary that was Reserve Stock.

He went into a newsagent's and purchased a box of left-over Starburst rockets. On the back, it said that this year's recipe contained a new chemical and produced a new colour, violet. It seemed altogether appropriate. Violet, the colour of ink stamps, rules and officialdom.

Midnight. He let himself in and went down the back stairs, opened one of the basement windows and left it ajar.

He took his cassette player along. He didn't have *Carmina Burana* but Tchaikovsky's *1812 Overture* did just as well. When everything was blazing and the books were curling and browning and dropping off the shelves like leaves in autumn, he went back upstairs and locked up. He left the empty box of rockets underneath the open window with plenty of burnt-out matches and a milk-bottle set into the earth.

Gradually, he reintroduced his escapees to the world, fitting them into second-hand bookshops, mainly down the Charing Cross Road, slipping them on to shelves when no one was looking, but he hung on to the book of prints. He didn't consider it theft.

'Is it theft,' he asked, 'to walk behind the bulldozers hunting sharp-eyed among the off-scourings, the parings and clippings, to walk over the crumpled moraine and lift an object clear? If there was a theft,' he said, 'it came before.'

He started a magazine with the redundancy money, publishing new writers in a paperback format. And Janice came back. She did the design and artwork while Harry was editor and chased up the authors. Janice wanted to call the magazine *Phoenix* but Harry said that was too obvious and so it became *The Day of the Dead*. Their distributors complained that it didn't sound Literary.

'It's a bit, well . . . black magic. You're not into all that, are you, Harry – voodoo, the occult?'

Esoteric? Yes, but it was also a pledge, and a prayer. When their first edition came out, a critic in one of the Sundays wrote, 'A dazzling debut, sheer pyrotechnics.' The cover featured a skeleton that sprouted leaves and flowers and, on the bones of its hand, a little brown bird, head back, singing.

Crime in a Fairy-tale Forest

▼

THERE IT IS, illuminated and sparkling, a ladder of lights, propped against the sky, the steepest hill in London, and I'm plodding up after a long day and late night at work, letting the frazzle of meetings, deadlines, phone calls, emails, leak into the February dark, walking slowly, too tired to hurry, the tail lights of the last bus sinking over the distant crest ahead, when I come across a spoon, as if the sickle moon above me has tipped, just a fraction, and a dribble of light has trickled over the edge and fallen through space, through time, to arrive at the tip of my shoe. A silver tablespoon on the pavement . . .

as if a burglar, with crêpe-soled shoes and woolly balaclava, going up the hill ahead of me, minding his business, had shifted his booty sack from one shoulder to the other and the spoon, finding a hole in the corner where a jagged object, perhaps a carriage clock, had rubbed at the hemp, slipped through, and just at that moment a police squad car, sirens blazing, hot on the trail of another burglar, swept by, tyres spraying droplets of oily rainwater into the cobbled gutter. (In this part of the city there are still cobbles under the tarmac, surfacing here and there at the edges.) And the burglar almost broke into a run, his heart banging dangerously, almost leapt into a hedge, but restrained himself at the last second because this wasn't the first time the cops had missed him, and in that tyre-squealing, siren-blazing instant, the cops missed him again and *he* missed the sound of silver striking tarmac, a thin note on a cold night, easily missed in the buzz of the city, so he went on, up the hill, and didn't notice that his sack was lighter by one spoon – an engraved silver spoon with a hallmark of a dancing bear, the date stamped into the underside of the handle – 1868 – Russian silver, scratched and worn . . .

as if a traveller in a tattered rabbit-fur hat and a greasy coat made of wolfskin had staggered through the hot, dusty streets of Constantinople, knocked on a wooden door studded with iron rivets and the butler, who worked for the British consul, opened it and asked him his business, but the traveller, burdened with state secrets, breathless and tear-stained, brushed past him and ran through another door, into a party, where women in low-cut evening gowns and masks twirled and glided on a polished floor in the arms of their escorts, while the band played, the chandeliers glittered, then the traveller trembled, lost his voice and fainted, recovering two days later to find himself tucked up in an attic, under a quilt embroidered with ducks, the contents of the little felt pouch he carried in his pocket exchanged for a bowl of chicken soup cooling by his bedside, the promise of the bed for one more night, none of which he understood because all he could hear were distant gunshots, footsteps crunching over frozen snow, while downstairs, in the basement pantry, the butler who was fussy about his cutlery, and fed up with all the polishing, sat on a high stool in front of an open window tossing out the remains of a once-treasured place setting – old-fashioned, the butler considered, and clumsy – so out it went, through the window to lie on the pavement, lonely without its fellows, lost, like a solitary crumb in a fairy-tale forest . . .

as if an old woman with a bent back, wicker shopping-trolley, flapping raincoat and transparent, pleated, plastic rain-hat, who took tea in the garden of the café at Kenwood House in Hampstead on a Monday afternoon when it was relatively quiet, in February, in the rain, who sat by the back wall, near the fig tree, and waited until no one was looking, or they'd all gone inside where it was altogether more cosy, less British, waited until she was alone. Then the old woman, who used to be a drug dealer in the nine-teen-sixties, who did time in Holloway and was released early on health grounds, slipped the spoon into her pocket. No doubt, thought the waiter (in Spanish), looking through the kitchen window, she will put that spoon into a drawer when she gets back home, along with a teaspoon from the Great Eastern Hotel at Liverpool Street, a dessert spoon from the Victoria and Albert Museum, all her other spoons, but he didn't care; he shrugged his shoulders and thought of his girlfriend back in Madrid, wondering when he would see her again and if they would one day be married and have children and grow as old as the old woman who was walking with difficulty over the flagstones, dragging her shopping trolley down the rain-sodden steps, slipping on the bottom one, the spoon falling out of her pocket, clinking, tip over tail, unnoticed by either of them, falling on to the pavement . . .

and I pick it up and put it in my pocket and run up the hill where the moon is still tipping over, and there is an echo, a thin note flying into the bosom of a million cars, a million CDs, radios, computer games, washing machines, a million people getting up to put on the kettle during the adverts, or during the scary bit, or the sexy bit, or the boring bit, and my legs have grown longer, my muscles stronger, and the night has grown larger . . .

Merete Morken Andersen OCEANS OF TIME   £8.99   ISBN 1 904559 11 5
A divorced couple confront a family tragedy in the white night of a Norwegian summer.
'A beautiful book' (Jostein Gaarder, author of *Sophie's World*), and a European bestseller.

Michael Arditti GOOD CLEAN FUN   £8.99   ISBN 1 904559 08 5
Twelve stories from the award-winning author of *Easter* provide a witty, compassionate yet
uncompromising look at love and loss, desire and defiance, in the twenty-first century.

Hélène du Coudray ANOTHER COUNTRY   £7.99   ISBN 1 904559 04 2
A prize-winning novel, first published in 1928, about a passionate affair between a British
ship's officer and a Russian emigrée governess which promises to end in disaster.

Lewis DeSoto A BLADE OF GRASS   £8.99   ISBN 1 904559 07 7
A lyrical and profound novel set in South Africa during the era of apartheid, in which the
recently widowed Märit struggles to run her farm with the help of her black maid, Tembi.

Maggie Hamand, ed. UNCUT DIAMONDS   £7.99   ISBN 1 904559 03 4
Unusual and sometimes challenging, these vibrant, original stories showcase the huge
diversity of new writing talent coming out of contemporary London.

Sara Maitland ON BECOMING A FAIRY GODMOTHER
£7.99   ISBN 1 904559 00 X
Fifteen new 'fairy stories' by an acclaimed master of the genre breathe new life into old
legends and bring the magic of myth back into modern women's lives.

Anne Redmon IN DENIAL   £7.99   ISBN 1 904559 01 8
A chilling novel about the relationship between Harriet, a prison visitor, and Gerry, a serial
offender, which explores challenging themes with subtlety and intelligence.

Dreda Say Mitchell RUNNING HOT   £8.99   ISBN 1 904559 09 3
Elijah 'Schoolboy' Campbell has just seven days to get out of London's underworld, where
bling, ringtones and petty deaths are accessories of life. An outstanding debut novel.

Henrietta Seredy LEAVING IMPRINTS   £7.99   ISBN 1 904559 02 6
Beautifully written and startlingly original, this unusual and memorable novel explores
a destructive, passionate relationship between two damaged people.

Norman Thomas THE THOUSAND-PETALLED DAISY
£7.99   ISBN 1 904559 05 0
Love, jealousy and violence play a part in this coming-of-age novel set in India, written
with a distinctive, off-beat humour and a delicate but intensely felt spirituality.

Adam Zameenzad PEPSI AND MARIA   £8.99   ISBN 1 904559 06 9
A highly original novel about two street children in South America whose zest for life
carries them through the brutal realities of their daily existence.